MYSTERY

Thumbprint Mysteries

NOT A CHANCE

BY

JUDITH ANDREWS GREEN

CONTEMPORARY BOOKS

a division of NTC/CONTEMPORARY PUBLISHING GROUP
Lincolnwood, Illinois USA

Thumbprint
Mysteries

MORE THUMBPRINT MYSTERIES

by Judith Andrews Green:

Hit the Street
Without a Trace

In memory of my father
Richard Lloyd Andrews

Cover Illustration: Alan Janson

ISBN: 0-8092-0683-8

Published by Contemporary Books,
a division of NTC/Contemporary Publishing Group, Inc.,
4255 West Touhy Avenue,
Lincolnwood (Chicago), Illinois 60646-1975 U.S.A.

90 QB 0 9 8 7 6 5 4 3 2 1

CHAPTER

1

Well, the classroom on the first floor of Kelly Hall didn't look like much that first evening in September. In fact the huge old building loomed dark and dismal, like the evil castle out of some late-night movie. But what could you expect? The whole of City College was badly in need of renovation.

Justin pushed his way through a small forest of plastic chair-and-desk combinations and threw himself into a seat near the front of the room. The fluorescent lights above him hummed.

Other students were shuffling into the classroom and taking seats around him. *Strange to think of myself as a student again*, Justin thought, *after all these years*. His daughter had started kindergarten last week, and here he was starting college. At last.

A desk scritched against the floorboards behind him as someone sat down heavily. Justin turned in his chair and held out a welcoming hand. "Hi! I'm Justin Cobb."

He was looking into a pair of eyes as flat and glossy as a couple of fried eggs. The eyes stared at him, unblinking, out of a round face, midwinter-pale. The man was not much older than Justin—early thirties, probably—although the plaid short-sleeved shirt buttoned across his heavy stomach made him seem somehow older. His hair was cut so short that it wouldn't lie down properly against his head, and a band of naked white skin arched over each ear. Justin noticed that his upper lip was beaded with sweat even though the classroom was on the cool side. The man's hands, soft and white like his face, stayed on his desktop gripping a fat, dog-eared notebook.

Justin tried again. "I'm a bit nervous—this is the first college course I've ever taken. How about you?" He shoved his hand forward again. In his six years as a used-car salesman, shaking hands was something he did without thinking.

Suddenly the man's hand floated up as if it had been pulled up on a string, and moist fingers touched Justin's palm. All five fingernails were chewed down to ragged stubs. "Remington Trask," the man said. His voice was not much more than a whisper.

"Well, Rem." Justin wanted to wipe his own hand against his pant leg, but he resisted the urge. "Are you going for a degree, or just taking this one course?"

"Remington," the man corrected, and then added in his almost soundless whisper, "I like math."

Two women of Justin's age came into the classroom, heading for chairs on the right. "Oh, hello!" one of them called to Justin. "I've seen you before. Aren't you Heather Cobb's husband?"

Justin turned toward her, glad for an excuse to give up this non-conversation with this giant sloth on two legs.

"That's me!" he told her. "Do you know Heather from the day care center?"

"Right. I'm Rachel Hylen, and my friend here is Stacy," she added, pointing to the other woman. "His wife run Little Friends Day Care where my son Allen goes," Rachel explained to Stacy. "It's just two blocks from here, over on Randall Street. Allen's been practically living there for the last two years, between my working and going to college." She threw her head back and laughed. "I've just got this math course to get through, and then I'm done! And I've got a great new job waiting for me when I get my degree!"

Meanwhile several younger men had straggled in and claimed the corner nearest the door. An older man threaded his way through the middle of the room, dropped into a chair directly under an open window, pulled out a big red bandana handkerchief, and an instant later exploded into a sneeze like a rifle shot. "'Scuze me," he muttered to no one in particular.

Now a man in a tweed jacket and dark green bow tie was bustling toward the teacher's desk at the front of the room. He whirled around and glared at the students from under bushy black eyebrows. "I'm Professor Quint!" he barked, as if daring them to argue with him. "This is Math 101. Are you all in the right place? Well, then, we'll take roll."

Justin tried to catch the names as they went by, but he was distracted by a chubby little man who rushed in, puffing, and plopped into a seat next to him. "Fred Whittaker," he announced to the professor.

"So nice of you to join us, Mr. Whittaker," Professor Quint snarled. "Now, if you are all quite ready—"

The classroom door opened again to admit a tall, thin young man with four thin silver hoops lined up in one ear. His taffy-colored hair was heaped up in the back as if something had been burrowing in it. He stalked across the classroom, jerked a chair slightly to the left with a nasty scraping sound, and dropped himself into it. A moment later his backpack clattered to the floor.

"And you must be—" Professor Quint made a great show of looking through his list "—James Shaner."

The silver earrings gleamed as the young man nodded once.

"Let's get started then. In this class, you will be learning mathematics. Now, mathematics has a beauty all its own, which you people are probably not smart enough to appreciate. You are probably just studying math so that you can learn to use a computer, right? You can't get away from the blasted things these days."

Quint glared out at his class, his eyes under the black eyebrows glittering like broken glass. "So before we can take up mathematics, I will have to teach you how to *think*. Therefore the first few classes will be taken up with the study of logic."

A restless sigh went through the room like a breeze rustling autumn leaves. *Logic!* Justin thought. *Now what have I got myself into?* Behind him, he could hear Remington Trask shift heavily in his chair. He could almost feel those fried-egg eyes glued to his back. He shuddered. At Wednesday night's class, he'd have to be sure to sit in the back, where he could keep an eye on Trask instead of the other way around.

"Now, in mathematics, we only deal with statements that can be proved true or false," Quint went on. "We don't deal with opinions. See here." He turned suddenly and snatched up a piece of chalk. The chalk rattled against the blackboard as he wrote:

Every triangle has three sides.

"This is a mathematical statement. It can be proved true or false. In fact, it happens to be true."

Over on the side of the room, the older man sneezed loudly into his bandana. Quint glared at him, then went back to writing on the blackboard as if he were attacking it.

Houston is a city.

Houston is the capital of California.

"These are both mathematical statements. Are you with me so far?"

No one dared to say no.

"What if I write this?" He looked for the blackboard eraser, spotted it at the far end of the chalk tray, impatiently rubbed out the first three sentences with his sleeve, and wrote:

It is cold in this room.

"What do you think?" he asked the blackboard. "Is this a mathematical statement? You, there." He whirled around and jabbed a stubby finger in the direction of the two women.

"Me?" Rachel squeaked. "I'm not sure—uh—yes?"

"No! No! It is *not* a mathematical statement!" Quint thundered. "But don't worry your pretty little head about it, you'll get it before long. We'll get one of the *men* to help you out." He pointed at Justin. "Can you tell us why it is *not* a mathematical statement?"

"Because it's a matter of opinion? It might seem cold to some people, but other people might think it's hot?" Justin said, visualizing the beads of sweat glistening along Remington Trask's upper lip.

"Exactly!" Quint sneered at Rachel. "Do you understand now?"

Rachel was rescued by another explosive sneeze from

over by the window. "Sorry, sorry," the man murmured into his bandana.

Then from the back row came a loud snore.

They couldn't help it. The whole class turned around. James Shaner had leaned his head on his hand and gone peacefully to sleep. In a moment, another racking snore droned out from under the heaped-up hair.

As one, the class faced forward to see Quint's reaction to this latest sacrilege. But Quint showed no sign of hearing the snores or noticing that he'd lost someone. "Let's look at double negatives. In logic, these two sentences mean the same thing," he said, and the chalk clattered against the chalkboard again as he wrote:

I don't have no money.

means

I have some money.

Justin stared at the two silly sentences on the blackboard. He had seven weeks to learn some algebra before he could take the physics and computer courses he was really interested in.

From the back corner of the classroom came another loud snore.

Behind Justin there was a chewing sound, and Justin knew that Remington Trask's fingernails were getting even shorter.

*   *   *

"Rachel Hylen was in my math class last night," Justin said as he reached across the kitchen table for the sugar bowl. "She says she's got a kid at Little Friends."

"Yes, she's one of my best customers," Heather said. "Come on, Casey, honey, open up. That's right!" She slipped a spoonful of cereal into the baby's mouth quick while it was open. "Who else was in your class?"

"Well, you should have seen the guy sitting behind me!"

Heather glanced up at his tone, then turned her eyes back to the baby. "What was wrong with him?" she asked.

"He was one of those real quiet, creepy guys," Justin said. "You know, the kind of guy no one ever notices. The kind of guy who goes to work every day and goes home every night to some little one-room apartment where he always pays the rent on time, and everything's fine. Then one day something just snaps inside, and the guy goes postal." Justin stirred a heaping spoonful of sugar into his coffee. "The guy gets a big gun and shoots a bunch of people in a fast-food restaurant, and all the neighbors say, 'I never knew him very well, but I never thought he'd—'"

"Justin! Stop it!" His wife lunged across the table to retrieve the sugar bowl from the baby's cereal-covered fingers. "Look! You've got Sarah all upset!"

"Sorry." Justin swiveled in his chair to look down at his five-year-old daughter. She was staring up at him while her spoonful of Cheerios dribbled a thin line of milk back into her bowl. She didn't look upset. She looked interested.

"Why would he do that, Daddy?" she asked. "Why would the man from your class kill people in a restaurant?"

"Oh, he wouldn't, sweetheart. I was just making a joke." Buying time, he took a big gulp of too-hot coffee. "Um—you should see the other people in the class," he told her. "The guy sitting next to me, his name was Fred. He had about ten pencils in his shirt pocket, all freshly sharpened and lined up in two neat rows like little soldiers. Only his stomach was so big that the pencils lay over sideways, like he was going to stick himself in the neck."

Sarah laughed and shoved the spoon into her mouth. "Who else was in your class?" she asked around a mouthful of Cheerios.

"Sarah, don't talk with your mouth full," Heather reminded her, but neither Justin nor Sarah looked up.

"Well, there were nine of us, all grown-ups," Justin said. "There was Rachel and another woman—they were just kind of ordinary-looking, not beautiful like your mother." Sarah's eyes turned toward Heather like car headlights. Heather flapped a hand and muttered something about flattery, but Justin could tell by the toss of her head as she reached to take the baby out of his high chair that she was pleased.

"Who else?" Sarah pressed.

"There was a young guy, real skinny and serious-looking like he spends so much time thinking about math that he doesn't remember to eat. He looked like he was trying get his hair to make dreadlocks, but he couldn't get it organized."

Sarah's eyebrows drew up like a pair of tiny feathers across her forehead. "Did he look nice?" she asked.

Justin thought a moment. "I don't remember his face very well. Right after the professor started speaking, he yawned really loudly, like this—" Justin demonstrated with a gut-wrenching gape, to a shriek of giggles from Sarah, and yawned a second time just for fun. "Then he plopped his chin into his hand and went to sleep." He leaned across the table and whispered to Sarah, "It didn't take long before he was *snoring*. You could tell that the professor was annoyed. He has big, bushy eyebrows, and anytime he was facing in the sleepy guy's direction, his eyebrows would crawl across the top of his nose like two big caterpillars having a conversation." Sarah rewarded Justin with another burst of giggles. "But the professor never said anything," Justin went on. "He just pretended the guy wasn't there."

"Why didn't someone else wake him up?" Sarah asked reasonably.

"Well, there was something about the way the professor was acting—as if he *wanted* the guy to make a fool of himself," Justin told her. "I don't know why. As far as I know, the professor hadn't met any of us before last night. The whole thing was kind of weird." Then he caught himself and added, "No, it was nothing. The guy had probably just stayed out late the night before. He needs to grow up!"

"When did you become such an old man?" Heather asked. As she passed behind his chair with the baby on her hip, she kissed him fondly on the top of his head where his scalp was beginning to show through his hair. "Come on, Sarah, finish your breakfast or you'll be late for kindergarten."

Sarah dug her spoon into her bowl. "Who else?"

"Well, there was one guy who sat all by himself over by the window, and he must have been allergic to the dust in the classroom, because he kept sneezing into a big red bandana handkerchief."

"Sneezy! I knew it!" Heather cried from the other side of the kitchen where she was washing the baby's face and hands in the sink. "Sneezy, Sleepy, Skinny, and Fred. Daddy's taking a math course with the seven dwarves!" She lugged the baby toward the doorway. "And this family's going to be late," she called in a singsong voice as she disappeared into the bedroom.

Justin glanced at his watch. "Yikes! Your mother's right! Mr. Manning's going to think I'm not properly excited about the idea of another day selling used sports cars!" He gulped his now-lukewarm coffee and grabbed for his suit jacket. "'Bye, sweetheart," he said as he kissed Sarah's warm curls. "Have a great day in kindergarten."

"Wait, Daddy!" Sarah said.

Justin looked down at her. Her face was tipped up toward his, her eyes large and serious. She was so tiny in the grown-up's chair that she had moved to when her baby brother had taken over the high chair that her round little chin barely cleared the rim of her cereal bowl. "What is it, honey?" he asked.

"Daddy, when someone shoots people in a *restaurant*, why do they call it going *postal*? It sounds more like he'd have to shoot them in the post office!"

Justin looked down at her, this precious little girl of his who always, always had one more difficult question to throw in his direction. Suddenly the face of Remington Trask pressed itself into his vision—the big, soft body, the sallow skin that made him look as if he lived in a basement somewhere, the flat, staring eyes.

As he nuzzled his face against the top of Sarah's head, enjoying the feeling of her warm curls against his cheek, he said a silent vow that he would keep his little girl out of post offices or fast-food restaurants or anyplace else necessary to keep her safe from that creep.

"No one's going to shoot anyone, sweetheart," he said. "I promise."

CHAPTER 2

Justin gazed out through the showroom window of Manning's Luxury Auto Sales at the parking lot where row upon row of shiny cars made identical lines and curves of hood and roof and trunk lid.

He was thinking about the way the air would flow over the cars. He could imagine the air slipping smoothly over the hood and up over the windshield and roof, then pressing down on the spoiler, keeping the car on the road, giving it better traction. He remembered how the wind would slide around him when he bent low over the handlebars of his racing bicycle. His legs pumped, and his body contracted into a coiled spring, and he and the bicycle shot forward as one—

He sighed.

He'd taken the sales job with Old Man Manning six years earlier when he and Heather were first married, soon after she found out she was pregnant with Sarah.

It had seemed like a good idea at the time even though it wouldn't bring in enough money for the house Heather was dreaming of. He'd felt like a solid citizen— it was certainly more responsible than his previous job as a bicycle messenger—and he figured it would pay the bills while he figured out what he really wanted to do with his life.

He was still trying to figure out what he wanted to do with his life. And he was still working for Old Man Manning.

And he hated every minute of it. Trapped inside the showroom all day, selling fast cars to other people, who drove them away to speed down the city streets and left him standing there in the dust.

God, how he missed those days when he was on his bicycle day after day, diving through traffic on the city streets. Everything was speed and freedom.

He propped his foot up against the windowsill that ran at shin height under the big showroom window and laid his elbow across his knee. His eyes ran over the front fender of the nearest Corvette in the parking lot, where the fender flared out over the wheel. He examined the precise angle of the lip over the tire, imagining the fender being tested in a wind tunnel for drag. His eyes narrowed. If he had designed that fender, he would have tried shortening the flare and lifting it a bit. He nodded, agreeing with himself. That would look much more stylish, and it ought to reduce the drag and give the car just that little edge of speed. He wished he could try his design in a wind tunnel.

Someday. Someday he would design these things and let someone else sell them.

The math class was supposed to be a start in that direction. If he were ever going to be an engineer, he knew he'd have to have a college degree. He had hoped to go to college when he and Heather were first married, but with Sarah coming along so soon and little Casey a few years later . . . Well, there'd never been time for college. Even with Heather running the Little Friends Day Care Center, there was no way he could quit his job and spend his time taking courses.

Then one day Heather had said, "But you could take one course."

And because City College had no evening courses that involved wind tunnels, he had started with math. He knew if he were going to design fast cars, he would need plenty of math.

Math. Justin sighed, staring out at the sleek shapes of the cars outside the showroom window. He couldn't see how the stuff Professor Quint had shown them in class last night was going to help him design cars. Maybe Mr. Dreadlocks snoring away in the back row had the right idea after all.

Justin snapped back into the world of car sales as a reflection of something behind him moved across the showroom window. He turned to face his boss.

The long narrow face cracked in half in what Old Man Manning thought was a smile. "Thinking of becoming a statue in City Park, Cobb?" he asked.

"Uh, no, Mr. Manning. I was just—"

"Keeping an eye on the merchandise in the parking lot, right? In case someone's trying to steal it? Good thinking, Cobb. I'm so glad we're paying you a salary for such high quality thinking."

"No, I—I mean—" In his six years of dragging himself around this joint, Justin had never figured out how to answer his boss's sarcasm.

"Right. Then if you have no prospects to call back, I suggest you put in some time checking invoices. We wouldn't want our customers to think there's nothing going on in here, would we?"

"Yes, sir. No, sir. Invoices it is, Mr. Manning." Justin scuttled toward the cubicle he shared with Tony Petrucelli and George Gomez, drawing a pen out of his breast pocket to demonstrate his extreme interest in checking those invoices the moment he hit his desk. *Wouldn't want our customers to think there's nothing going on!* His boss's words danced through his head. *What customers?* he wanted to shout. *There's no one in here right this moment! Why do we always have to pretend the place is full of customers?*

He settled down at his desk and pulled a stack of invoices out of his in-basket. He checked the first one against the printout, then reached for the second one.

Manning's footsteps clicked past the cubicle in the precise line between the showroom window and his own office doorway.

Justin let the second invoice drift down to the desktop. He was safe for the moment, as long as he stayed in the cubicle. Old Man Manning was a creature of habit. His quota was always one chewing-out per morning. *Lightning,* his employees always said, *doesn't strike twice in the same spot.*

Justin listened to the voices beyond the partition that separated him from the showroom. It sounded as if Tony had a customer. George was just chatting with Penny Koch, the receptionist. George and Penny were lucky that Justin had drawn Manning's fire before they did.

He glanced over at George's desk. The morning newspaper was set on the corner, neatly folded as if it were waiting, unread, for George's lunch hour. Justin

knew better. When he unfolded it and looked inside, he
found the sports section was folded in backwards. Sure
enough, George had been sneaking a peek at the scores
from last night's games. The pennant race was heating up.

Justin slid the sports section out of the newspaper and
tucked it into George's bottom desk drawer, where
George might find it in two or three days if he was lucky.
As Justin refolded the rest of the paper again and laid it
back on George's desktop, he glanced at the headline on
the bottom of the page. DEBATE RAGES AT CITY
COLLEGE, the headline said, and under that, in smaller
print, DAY CARE CENTER OR FACULTY CLUB?

City College? A day care center at City College
would mean real competition for Heather's place. He
opened the newspaper out across George's desk and
leaned over it.

*The completion of the new Franklin Administrative
Building at City College has led to a heated debate over
what to do with the recently vacated administrative offices
in the old facility in Eastman Hall. A student group,
Students for a Fair Shake, are urging the college to turn at
least part of the facility into a day care center for the
children of students attending the college. Some members of
the faculty, however, led by math professor Augustus Quint,
feel that the area should be used for badly needed office
space for college faculty and staff, as well as a faculty club.*

Justin whistled. Stumping for a private club for faculty
sounded just like something his math professor would do.
But another day care center—

The student who was the organizer of Students for a
Fair Shake had raised the ante, according to the article, by
publicly accusing Quint of being a snob who didn't give
a hoot about the community. Quint evidently made it
clear he didn't appreciate the accusation; in fact, he

suggested that he was consulting his lawyer to see if the statement could be considered libelous. *Hot times at City College*, Justin thought.

At the end of the article was a small photograph of Professor Quint in a jacket and tie, probably taken from the college's files. Beside it was a slightly fuzzy photograph of an angry-looking young man in semi-dreadlocked hair. *James Shaner of Students for a Fair Shake*, read the caption under the picture.

Justin gawked at the photograph. Even slightly out of focus, there was no doubt that the young man in the picture was the rude snorer in the back row of the math class. Shaner had carried the debate into Professor Quint's classroom. This was going to be an interesting term!

"Well, well, Cobb," said a sharp voice next to his ear, "I see you're making wonderful progress with those invoices! I'm beginning to wonder whether or not you want to continue to work here."

Justin straightened up and found himself staring straight into the barrel of Old Man Manning's best glare.

Lightning, he found, did sometimes strike twice in the same spot.

*   *   *

The day was winding down at Little Friends Day Care. Only a few children remained to be picked up. Laurie, the part-time help who came in to cook the children's lunch and prepare the snacks, had long since tidied up the kitchen and gone home. Nellie, Heather's assistant, was pulling on her raincoat. Nellie, tiny and quiet and absolutely indispensible, had been willing to shift her schedule when Sarah started kindergarten so that Heather could take Sarah to school in the morning. Nellie opened up and received the earliest children in the morning; Heather stayed until all the stragglers were gone and closed up. The new schedule seemed to be working out beautifully.

"Good night, Heather," Nellie called, lifting her long, dark braid over the collar of her raincoat to let it fall in its neat, straight line down the center of her back. "See you tomorrow."

"Good night." Heather watched her pull open the bright red front door and step out into the slanting afternoon rain. Nellie had gone from her usual shy reserve to something resembling total silence. Something must be bothering her, but until and unless Nellie chose to share it, Heather would never know what it was.

She got Sarah and the three other temporarily leftover children to help her pick up the rest of the toys in the main room. Then she set them to coloring quietly at the big table in the corner while she waited for their parents to arrive. Casey kicked his feet contentedly in his high chair, alternately watching them and playing with a set of plastic measuring spoons. With everything peaceful for the moment, Heather went into the kitchen to see if Laurie had left her a shopping list for tomorrow's snacks.

She looked through the slips clipped together under a big magnet on the refrigerator and checked the supply of bread in the freezer. She turned, running her eyes along the worn Formica counter, looking for Laurie's list. A motion at the window made her look up sharply.

What was that?

Something had been there. She had seen nothing more than a pale blur. A face? *Something* had been there.

She stood immobile for an instant, grasping the edge of the counter in both hands. Then she forced herself to walk toward the window and look out into the alley.

There was no one there. There was nothing in the alley

except her car with Casey's child seat poking up in the backseat.

She rubbed her hand over her eyes. She was getting tired, that was all. "Mama," Sarah said from the doorway, "Vanessa's mother is here."

"Coming, darling," Heather said. She took one more long look down the alley, then headed for the main room to see Vanessa into her jacket and gone.

She tried not to think about it when, half an hour later, she gathered up her own children, opened the back door, and stepped with them out into the alley. But when Sarah asked to be allowed to practice opening the car door with the key, Heather snapped, "Not tonight!" On her hip, Casey wriggled restlessly, annoyed at being held too tightly. She hastened to buckle the children into their places, then relocked the doors before starting the car. Sarah looked at her questioningly, but she seemed to know by instinct that this was not a good time to ask her mother to explain her actions.

They drove the few blocks home in silence, but as they pulled into the alley behind their apartment building, Sarah said, "You said we were going to go to the grocery store!"

"Not tonight, sweetheart," Heather said. "We'll have to make do with what we've got at home." She parked the car in its usual spot, well away from the piles of wood scraps and cement bags that marked the construction next door. When would they ever get that project finished? It seemed as if they'd been working on that building for months!

She lifted Casey out of his car seat and, shepherding Sarah ahead of her, she mounted the back steps, slippery from the afternoon rain. She fumbled her key out of her pocketbook and opened the back door. As she approached the staircase, she shook her head in exasperation. A string of muddy footprints led from the front door to the staircase.

Must be one of the new tenants, she thought. Justin would never let the good shoes that he wore to work get as muddy as that.

Step by step up the stairs, the mud had begun to wear off, but as she mounted, lugging Casey, she could still see traces of it. The mud preceded her across the landing, passed the new tenant's door, and continued up the second flight of stairs.

Heather began to feel a bit nervous. The possibilities were beginning to get narrowed down.

Sure enough, the mud marched right across the third-floor landing up to her door. *There can be only one person . . .*

Before Sarah could reach for the buzzer, the door popped open on its own and a pair of arms swooped down and scooped her up. "Hugo!" she squealed. "Oh, Hugo, it's you! It's you with the muddy feet!"

"Hi, Hugo," Heather said, pushing past him to put Casey down on the rug before he wriggled out of her arms completely. "It's good to see you. Where's Nellie?"

"Um. She didn't come with me," Hugo said.

"What's going on with you guys?" Heather asked. "Nellie seemed sort of upset at work, and you don't look so good either."

Actually, with Hugo it was somewhat hard to tell. His hair, although neatly trimmed, had a tendency to spring away from his head in different directions, giving him a look as if a company of small tornadoes had come by recently and twisted his hair into a series of individual knots. His sweater sagged off his bony shoulders, and his pants hung from his belt like wet laundry on a line. This was Hugo at his best.

But for those who knew him well, the clues were there. His face, usually as happy as a small boy with a double-decker ice cream cone, was drawn and pinched. And he had gone back to his favorite old pink high-top sneakers, one tied with a fuzzy, neon-green lace and the other held shut with a paper clip, both still covered with drying mud. *I wonder why Nellie never got rid of those sneakers*, Heather thought. *Hugo must have hidden them for an emergency like this.*

Sarah wrapped her arms around Hugo's neck and laid her cheek against his. "What's the matter, Hugo?" she asked.

When Hugo looked at Heather, his eyes were lined up exactly with Sarah's. "Nellie threw me out," he said simply. "Can I stay here with you guys for a while, just till things blow over?"

Heather looked past him into the living room where Justin sat on the couch with his long legs stretched out in front of him. He shrugged. "When I got home, he was sitting on the front steps. I couldn't leave him out there in the rain, could I?"

"Oh, Mama, please! He can have my bed!" Sarah pleaded.

"Of course you can stay with us, Hugo," Heather said. "But shouldn't you call Nellie and—"

"She won't talk to me." Hugo pressed his forehead against Sarah's. "Owl eyes! Owl eyes!"

Sarah shrieked with laughter, and down on the rug Casey crawled over to Hugo's legs and bellowed to be picked up so he could join in the fun.

*   *   *

Somehow, supper got cooked and eaten. It seemed to take forever to get the kids bathed and ready for bed. Even after she had been tucked in for the night, Sarah ran out into the living room holding her teddy bear while Heather was making up a bed for Hugo on the couch. "I just wanted to give Hugo Mimi to sleep with," she said, "so he won't be all alone out here." Heather never thought to tell Justin about the fright she'd had at the end of the day at Little Friends. And it was close to ten o'clock before Justin got a chance to tell Heather about James Shaner's push for a day care center at City College.

Heather stopped in her tracks in the middle of the living room floor, an extra blanket for Hugo dangling from her arm. "A day care center at the college?" she gasped. "But that's only a few blocks from Little Friends! A lot of our parents are students at the college! We could lose a lot of customers! If they have a building right on campus, they wouldn't have to pay rent or heat or anything! We could never compete with that! Did the newspaper say—"

Justin knew what she was going to ask next. "Yes, the newspaper said that Shaner wants this day care to be open to everyone in the neighborhood if there's room."

Heather groaned. She plopped down on the couch and put her face in her hands. "We're just barely making it as it is," she said. "If we lose all our best customers, we won't be able to stay open! It's not fair! I've tried so hard at Little Friends! It's not fair!"

"Maybe it won't happen," Justin said. "According to the paper, Quint and his gang are dead set against it. Shaner's that guy from my math class, the one who was snoring last night," he said. "I guess he was just giving Professor Quint a hard time."

"If we close," Heather wailed, "you watch—City

College won't be able to take all the children. Some of the families will be left without anyone to look after their children. People will lose their jobs!" She pounded her fists against her knees. "I hope Professor Quint wins! *Somebody* has to stop that Shaner guy!"

Suddenly she stopped. There was an odd sound coming from the kitchen.

Framed in the doorway, she could see Hugo dumping Cheerios into a bowl, higher and higher until they formed a small mountain. Now more Cheerios were rolling down the sides of the mountain and cascading onto the floor, and still he poured. Even from the living room, Heather could hear the Cheerios crunch crisply under his feet as he righted the box and stepped over to the counter to set it down. Beyond him, the refrigerator door yawned open.

Without noticing what she was doing, Heather picked up Sarah's teddy bear and threw it hard against the living room wall.

CHAPTER
3

The next morning when Heather had tried to wake Hugo for work, he just threw a skinny arm over his eyes and groaned. He usually worked for one or another of Nellie's cousins, but on this particular morning he seemed to have no particular destination.

Heather had just shrugged and left him on the couch. "Nellie must have run out of cousins," she told Justin.

Justin hurried to get home from work ahead of Heather that afternoon, just in case. A "murmph" from the living room led him to where Hugo was hunched in front of the computer on the desk in the corner, playing hearts at lightning speed. He didn't look up.

Justin loosened his tie and yanked it off by one end while he looked around the room. The apartment was already beginning to have that Hugo look. A banana peel lay open like a starfish across the arm of the couch. A stack of magazines had slumped from the end table onto the floor. An empty cereal bowl sat perched on the very edge of the desk, just waiting to topple.

Sighing, Justin took a moment to roll up the tie in his long, slim fingers and shove it in his pocket before setting to work to kill the evidence of Hugo's day in the living room. Then he spent the next half hour finishing up his assignment for his math course, a set of sentences Professor Quint had given them to correct. He sat carefully counting out the pairs of *no*'s in

It isn't true that there's not no such thing as a unicorn.

It was sort of interesting, he had to admit, but he couldn't see how it was going to help him design fast cars.

He heard Heather come in with the kids. He cocked an ear toward the living room, but all the noises seemed to be happy ones. When he came into the kitchen a few minutes later, Heather was just putting some take-out Chinese food on the table, Hugo was romping around the living room rug with Sarah astride his back, and from his high chair Casey waved his arms and chortled with glee. Maybe having Hugo here would work out. For a while.

But when Heather turned to face him, her face was etched with worry. "I tried to talk to Nellie today," she began.

"About Hugo?"

"Oh, it looked as if she knew Hugo was here. She didn't seem to care one way or the other. But when I told her about that grand scheme for a day care center at the college, she already knew about it! She told me that your James Shaner is someone she knew from high school— and he's offered her a job! Listen to this: he told her that if they're successful in getting the day care center going at the college, she can be the director!" Heather slammed down the little white cardboard box she'd been holding so hard that a geyser of pork fried rice shot upwards and sprayed across the table. "Come and eat, everyone," Heather bellowed.

Hugo was tossing Sarah up into the air. "Higher! Higher!" Sarah shrieked. "I want to touch the ceiling!"

Justin sat down at the table and began to scrape clumps of rice from the center of the table onto his plate. "I feel bad leaving you here alone with all this while I go to class," he told Heather.

They both knew he was lying.

*　　*　　*

When Justin got to the classroom, he lingered in the doorway until Remington Trask plodded by, clutching his worn notebook. When Trask had settled himself into the same chair he had sat in on Monday evening, Justin chose a chair behind him and to the side, so that he could see the professor without having to look at Trask.

He watched the others come in: Fred, still armed with a pocketful of pencils; Rachel and the other woman, looking angry; the man who sneezed. In ones and twos, the students dribbled into the classroom. Justin looked around for James Shaner, wondering what he would pull tonight to annoy Quint. Shaner was not yet there.

At the stroke of seven o'clock, Quint popped through the door, strode straight toward the blackboard as if he were alone in the room, and wrote:

If an animal is a dog, then it has four legs.

"True or false?" he snapped. "Quickly!"

"True!" called out the man with the bandana.

"What about this one?"

If an animal does not have four legs,
then it is not a dog.

There was a moment's hesitation. Quint rapped his chalk against the blackboard. "Come on, come on, people. This is not rocket science!"

Justin drew his hand over his eyes. Quint was beginning to sound just like Old Man Manning. "True," someone said, and the rest of the class murmured agreement.

"Is it safe to say that this statement is true backward and forward?" Quint asked. "What about this one? And this?"

If an animal has four legs, then it is a dog.

If an animal is not a dog,
then it does not have four legs.

"False!" called out a voice from the doorway. "A proposition and its converse are not necessarily equivalent." Justin turned to see James Shaner stalk in and take a seat. "The inverse does not necessarily follow, either," he added.

"Ah, Mr. Shaner!" Quint's eyes were hard, bright little beads under the black fur of the eyebrows. "You have been reading ahead! What a good student you are!" He rubbed his hands together, brushing off the chalk dust. "Let's see what else you have learned."

The man by the window sneezed loudly. "'Scuze me," he muttered. Quint didn't even glance in his direction

The next hour of the class became a battle of wits between Shaner and Quint. "Mr. Shaner!" Quint called out. "True or false: If blue isn't green and if blue isn't not red, then it is false that it's not true that it's not the case that blue isn't not purple."

Justin understood enough to know what James Shaner was doing when he rapped back "False!" but he had no idea how Shaner could do it without a pencil and paper.

But even as the sentences got longer and longer, Quint never caught him out. How could he get them right so quickly? Or *was* he getting them right—did Quint even know if they were right or not?

For this Justin had given up an evening with his family?

When Quint called time for a break, the entire group was out of the classroom like a shot. Even the non-smokers joined the huddle around the front door. Only James Shaner stood by himself in the hallway, calmly looking over his notes. And Remington Trask, of course, had disappeared somehow in the general stampede for the door, looking out at the mist that had enveloped the city when the rain stopped.

"Well, I've had enough," said a young man in a Green Bay Packers sweatshirt. "I've got better things to do tonight."

"Yeah!" Rachel's friend exclaimed. "Why should I pay a babysitter so I can listen to this old chauvinist have some kind of weird argument with that guy with the earrings, just because the guy fell asleep in class on Monday?"

"No, no, it's more than that, Stacy!" the other woman said. "Didn't you see yesterday's newspaper? Professor Quint wants to turn Eastman Hall into a faculty club, and that guy with the earrings wants it to be a student union."

"Well," Fred said nervously, "I guess we should be getting back to class."

"What do you think, Rachel?" Stacy asked. "Are you going back in?"

Rachel considered for a long minute. "Yeah," she said at last. "I need this math credit."

That seemed to decide them all. Even the young man in the Packers sweatshirt joined the group that followed Shaner back into the classroom.

Quint was at the front of the room drawing some kind of chart on the blackboard while Trask slumped in his seat watching him, his soft, white hands wrapped around his precious notebook.

"These are truth tables," Quint announced. "To save space, we use symbols. Let us call this sentence p," he said, and wrote on the board,

   p *Abraham Lincoln was our sixteenth president.*

"To make this statement false, we add this symbol, which means *not p*," and he wrote:

   $\sim p$ *Abraham Lincoln was not our sixteenth president.*

"Now, at the top of the truth table we write the two symbols, p and $\sim p$, and then mark the spaces below T if the statement is true, and F . . ." As Quint talked happily to the blackboard, Justin felt his eyelids grow heavy.

He was working in a lab, standing over a drafting table, the plans for the newest Jaguar convertible laid out before him. It was going to be a great car, sleek and faster than ever before. There was just one little problem with the drag over the rear fenders, and if Justin could just solve it, the car would be perfect. He hurried over to the computer and tapped on a few keys. On the computer screen, the three-dimensional view of the car turned smoothly this way and that. Justin studied the screen intently, made a few calculations . . .

Justin jerked awake as a loud snore sounded through the classroom. *Had it been him?* He glanced around at the back row and was relieved to see that Shaner's hawklike face had disappeared once more into his hand. A moment later another snore filled the air.

Justin settled down in his seat again and wondered if it was too late to get his money back. Probably. He'd chosen the seven-week fast-track class so he could get another course in before Christmas, so he was probably already past the cut-off for a refund.

Justin propped his chin in his hand and gazed at Quint's desk, littered with a mess of books and papers that Hugo could have been proud of. In the center of the desk, as if Quint wanted to be very sure that it couldn't fall off, was a large black instrument—a calculator, Justin assumed, although it was like no other calculator Justin had ever seen before. For one thing, it had about a dozen more buttons on it than the one he kept in his desk at work. There was a small screen at one end, making the whole thing look more like a hand-held computer. *I wonder what that thing will do?* Justin mused. *I'll bet that's the kind of thing I really should be learning about.*

When ten o'clock finally came and Quint dismissed the class, Justin lingered, hoping for a look at that calculator. Shaner was gone in a moment, followed quickly by the young man in the Packers sweatshirt and more slowly by the man who sneezed. He stuffed his bandana into his pocket, smiled at the floor, and shuffled out, saying, "'Scuze me, 'scuze me." Trask lumbered out, clutching his notebook. Stacy headed for the door, then turned as she realized that Rachel was still at her seat, gathering up her papers.

Justin stepped up to Quint, who was tossing the books and papers from the desk into a battered briefcase. "What is it? What is it?" Quint demanded. "Speak up!"

"This calculator—" Justin began.

"That's a graphing calculator. Very expensive!" Quint barked as he saw Justin's hand reaching toward it. "We won't be using it in this course, but I just don't like leaving it in my office. The locks in this old building aren't that great."

"What will it do?" Justin asked. He was aware of Fred behind him, peering over his shoulder. "You see, I'm taking this course to prepare myself to—"

"It'll do almost anything," Quint cut him off, "*if* you know how to use it. Now if you'll excuse me—"

"Professor Quint," Rachel put in, "do you have any handouts on that inverse and converse stuff? I was trying to take notes, but I really couldn't keep up with you."

Quint's eyebrows met in a dark scowl, but he dug through his briefcase. "I've got some stuff in my office," he said, shoving the last of the papers from the desk into his briefcase. "Follow me in there, and I'll get it for you. Here!" He shoved a small pamphlet at Justin. "You gentlemen are welcome to look through the instruction booklet while I'm gone, but don't touch the calculator! I don't want you bungling around and messing up any of the function keys. Come on, miss! Let's see if we can straighten you out."

Followed by Rachel and at more of a distance by Stacy, Quint stalked out of the classroom. Justin flipped open the instruction booklet. Fred, from behind his picket fence of pencils, strained to see over his shoulder, so Justin laid it out on the desktop and turned the pages slowly.

This would be a great calculator to have, he could see that. Most of the math was beyond him, but he was sure that in time he could learn it. Math had always come more easily to him than anything involving reading.

They reached the last page, and Justin closed the booklet and laid it carefully next to the calculator. Quint had not yet returned. "Guess we'd better stay here and guard the machine," he told Fred.

Fred nodded.

The fluorescent lights hummed.

"So, Fred, why are you taking this class?" Justin asked. "Are you working on a degree?"

Fred nodded. "I hope so," he said.

Out on the street, a truck rattled past.

Justin walked to the doorway and looked down the hallway. He could see a crack of light under one of the doors. That must be Quint's office. But the door was shut. Rachel must still be in there asking questions. Maybe she was trying to convince Quint to move on to some algebra.

He turned back to the classroom. Fred stood right where he had left him among the empty chairs with his pencils standing at attention in his pocket.

"Look, Fred," Justin said, "we both don't have to stand here. Why don't you go ahead, and I'll just stick around until Quint comes back for his precious calculator."

"Well—" Fred looked at his wristwatch. "I guess—"

"Go ahead," Justin urged. "Quint will be along any second."

"Okay." Fred waddled out the door. A moment later Justin heard the front door open and close.

He settled down to look over the assignment Quint had given them. It went on for pages. Well, he might as well get started.

As he worked through the first page, he found that the truth tables made more sense as he went along, but he really had to concentrate. He moved on to the second page.

What time was it, anyway? He checked his watch: way past ten-thirty, for crying out loud! Heather was going to think he'd died or something! Well, he'd just have to break in on Rachel's meeting with Quint and give this calculator back, so he could go home. Quint wouldn't break his arm if he just picked the darned thing up and carried it down the hall.

Justin packed up his papers, stuck the instruction booklet into his pocket, then gingerly picked up the calculator. He shut out the classroom lights and stepped out into the hallway.

The hallway lights were still on, shining grimly on the dingy paint of the walls and on the long, narrow, well-scuffed floor, but down the corridor, no lights gleamed. Quint's office was dark. The building was silent.

What a jerk! Justin huffed to himself. *Quint forgot all about his darned calculator and left me sitting there while he took off and went home!* Justin tried to feel angry as he walked down the corridor, hearing his footsteps echo like the sound track of a horror movie. But what he really felt was uneasy as he approached the door where he'd seen the light on half an hour ago. Sure enough, the plastic nameplate said *A. Quint.* Justin raised his hand to knock on the door.

There had been a time years ago when he had been sent to deliver a package at an office downtown. He had knocked at the door, and there had been no answer. The next morning in the newspaper he had understood why. The man the package was addressed to had been lying on the floor on the other side of that door while Justin had been knocking on it. And the man had been dead.

That was a long time ago, Justin told himself as he rapped once, twice, three times under the plastic nameplate. *That was a whole different situation.*

But he wasn't going to wait around in that silent corridor. Quickly he tore a page from his notebook and scribbled a note.

Professor Quint—

I waited in the classroom for you, but you didn't come back for your calculator. I've taken it home with me for safekeeping, and I'll bring it back to you

*tomorrow. If you need to reach me, my home phone is
555-3674 and my work phone at Manning's Auto
Sales is 555-2100.*

—Justin Cobb

He shoved the note under the office door, then turned
and walked down the corridor, listening to the hollow
echo of his own footsteps and holding the calculator out
in front of him like a carton of eggs.

He had told himself over and over as he walked the
four blocks to his own street that this was a whole
different situation from that other time—but still he was
not surprised to hear the first of the police sirens.

He stopped on the sidewalk in the soft September
mist to listen.

The siren was headed toward City College.

CHAPTER 4

As if he were walking in his sleep, Justin followed the sound of the siren toward City College.

An ambulance was backed up to the front door of Kelly Hall, its revolving light cutting through the mist. A police car sat diagonally across the front walk, and two policemen were holding back the crowd that had already begun to gather.

"What's going on?" Justin asked a young couple who were standing near the police car with their arms around each other.

"Some professor bought it," the young man said. "The custodian found him in his office."

"We saw him!" his girlfriend said, her eyes wide and innocent under their dark circles of mascara. "The custodian was too whacked-out to use the phone in the dead guy's office. He came tearing out here yelling for help, so we called 911 from the front lobby, and then—"

"We thought we'd have a look," the young man said. He was trying to act as if he saw dead bodies every day of the week, but his voice was shaking. "The custodian thinks he had a heart attack."

"Who was it?" Justin asked. "Do you know his name?"

The young man looked at his girlfriend. "The custodian said—do you remember?"

"Quint?" Justin cut in. "Was it Professor Quint?"

"Yeah!" the young man said. "That was the name, wasn't it, Jessie?"

Jessie shrugged. "I guess so. There was *blood!*"

"His head was kind of bashed on one side. Must've hit it when he fell," the young man explained.

"So we called 911," Jessie said, "and they came right away, just like on television. It was cool!"

"But I was just in Quint's class! Tonight! He was teaching us logic!"

"Yeah, well, I guess you're going to have to find a new teacher," the young man said.

Suddenly Justin couldn't bear to be there anymore. He turned away and pushed his way through the people who were gathering around the police car. By the time he got to the street, he was almost running.

It wasn't until Heather asked him what he had in his hand that he remembered he was still holding the calculator.

*   *   *

He sat up late talking to Heather and Hugo. It was kind of nice, having Hugo there. He'd been through a lot with them in the past. It felt like a good backup, having him around now.

"I just can't get it through my head!" Justin said. "I was sitting there in his classroom, doing the homework he had just assigned, and he was fifty feet away down the hallway—dead! Just like that! It really makes you think."

"But you think it was a heart attack, right?" Heather asked. "Even though that kid said there was blood on his face?"

"Yeah, it must have been a heart attack," Justin said. "The guy was a real jerk, the angry type. He was a heart attack just waiting to happen. Right?" He looked at Heather and then at Hugo, his shoulders and hands lifted in an appeal. "He thought he was better than anyone else. He was sarcastic to his students. But you don't *kill* a guy for being sarcastic, right?"

"Just in case, don't you think you'd better call the police and tell them you were there?" Heather asked.

"No," Justin said. "I don't have anything to tell them."

*   *   *

The police thought otherwise.

"Oh, Mr. Cobb," Penny Koch called to him the next afternoon from the reception desk just inside the showroom window, "come here a second, would you?"

"Sure." Justin walked briskly toward her, knowing from her use of his last name that Mr. Manning was within hearing distance.

"You had a call a couple of hours ago, but you were busy, and then I forgot to give you the message. I have the slip here somewhere." She was rummaging around in the snowstorm of papers on her desk. "The guy was sort of strange. I could hardly hear what he was saying—he spoke in a kind of whisper—and he wouldn't leave his name. He said—"

Justin hardly heard her. A police car had just pulled

into the parking lot in front of the showroom. Its doors swung open and two policemen stepped out, straightened up like springs uncoiling, and stood looking up at the big sign over the front door.

The two policemen seemed a poor match. One was well past fifty with a comfortable stomach and a deeply tired look in his eyes, as if he'd seen too much in his years on the police force. The other was younger than Justin, athletic. His arms swung easily at his sides as he paced toward the front door. His face was hard and alert.

Justin's legs quivered under him with the urge for action. He'd give anything to slide out the back door and make a run for it. Instead, he took the message slip from Penny and forced himself to walk slowly into his cubicle where he sat down at his desk across from George and waited.

Tony Petrucelli ushered the two policemen into the cubicle, his face a careful blank. "Are you Justin Cobb?" the younger policeman asked. His voice was deep and rough, as if being Justin Cobb was a crime in itself.

George glanced up from his newspaper, gasped, and melted away, leaving his newspaper spread out on his desk. The other policeman sat down in the chair he had abandoned and asked, "You are taking a course at City College taught by Professor Augustus Quint?"

Justin nodded.

"I'm Officer Mosher, and this is Officer Sawicki. We are investigating the death of Professor Quint," he said. "We have information that you were at the class he taught last night just before he was found dead." The policeman took out a tiny notebook and looked into it as if it could help him pretend he was somewhere else. Officer Sawicki took up a position behind his chair with his feet planted firmly and his arms folded behind his back. He was watching Justin carefully. "We have been interviewing the members of the class," Officer Mosher went on, "to find out if anyone saw or heard anything unusual."

"No," Justin said. He fought to stay calm, but his heart was pounding so hard that he thought the policemen must be able to hear it. "No, I didn't hear anything. The building was quiet. I was in the classroom, and Professor Quint was in his office with a student. Down the hall. His office was down the hall. From the classroom. When I went looking for him, the office was dark, and I knocked, but there was no answer, so I thought he'd gone home." He realized he was talking faster and faster. He took a deep breath and let it out slowly. "So I left," he added. "It was a heart attack, right? There wasn't anything else, like a robbery or anything?"

Officer Mosher had his notebook again, slowly flipping through one page after another. "His wallet was in his pocket, untouched," he said in a sad voice. "When Mrs. Quint came to his office, she could identify only one or two things that were missing. If there was a robbery, the perpetrator did not have time to complete it." He looked up at Justin, and his eyes were suddenly hard. "Why do you ask?"

"Well, I—I was just wondering, because, well, he'd hit his head, right? And I was thinking that maybe—"

"That's interesting," Officer Mosher said. "We never mentioned that he'd had a blow to the head. It's very interesting that you should bring it up."

"But—but that's what they said—Jessie and her boyfriend." Frantically Justin tried to remember if he'd heard the boyfriend's name. "They told me—"

Officer Sawicki cut in impatiently, "According to another student we spoke with, a Mr. Fred Whittaker, you were the last one to leave the classroom."

"That's right. I was waiting for Professor Quint, but he didn't come back—"

"And you heard no one?" Officer Sawicki pressed.

"Well, there was someone upstairs—I heard a clanking sound, like maybe a mop in a bucket. I didn't pay much attention. I guess I figured it was the custodian." Justin appealed to the older policeman. "Wasn't it the custodian who found Professor Quint?"

Officer Mosher gazed at his notebook as if it were a crystal ball. "Yes, the custodian found him," he finally admitted. "So you knocked on his door—" He laid the notebook down on top of George's newspaper and pulled a pen out of his pocket. He adjusted his glasses and prepared to write. "You knocked on his door—" he said again.

"And no one answered, so—"

"Wait a minute. Wait a minute." Oficer Mosher patted down the newspaper. "There's something under here, I can't write."

He folded back the newspaper. A black, rectangular object lay on the desktop, glistening with buttons. Justin and the two policemen all stared at it. "What is this thing?"

Justin's throat tightened over the words until they came out as a squeak: "It's—um, it's a special math calculator. It's—" He had to push the words out. "It belongs to Professor Quint."

Officer Mosher looked up at Justin where he stood backed into the corner of his cubicle, and his eyes were deeply sad. "And how do you happen to have this calculator?"

"Professor Quint said I could look at it. I went to take it to his office, but like I said, I thought he was gone, and

I knew he wouldn't want me just to leave it in the classroom where someone might take it, so I took it—I mean I took it home to take care of it, if you know what I mean. I wrote him a note and told him I was going to bring it back to him today, and I shoved it under the door to his office."

"You wrote him a note," Officer Sawicki said.

"Yes, so he wouldn't worry when he got there this morning. And I was going to take it back to the college on my way home from work. I mean, I knew I couldn't give it to *him*, because he was dead—"

"Oh, so you knew he was dead." Officer Mosher made a note.

"Yes, I told you, I was going home last night and I heard the sirens, so I went back to the college—"

"Interesting," said the younger policeman. "Very interesting."

Justin wanted to weep, listening to the calm repetition of that word *interesting*. "So I brought the calculator to work with me, so I could take it to the college on the way home like I said, and George—that's his desk—George must have been looking at it—" Justin's words tumbled out like marbles clattering down a chute. He was terribly aware that his mouth was working about five times as fast as his brain.

"Well, Mr. Cobb," Officer Mosher said. He carefully stowed his pen and notebook in his shirt pocket and dragged himself to his feet. "I guess you'll have to come to the police station with us and make a more complete statement."

"But—I've already told you I didn't see anyone! So why—"

"There are some parts of your story that don't check out very well," Officer Sawicki said. "The calculator, for one thing. Mrs. Quint noticed right away that it was missing. She says it's worth a considerable amount of money and would be quite valuable to the right person. A math student, for example."

"But I told you! I left him a note!"

Officer Mosher shook his head sadly. "I'm sorry, son. We've been through that office with a fine-tooth comb." He reached out one large hand and took Justin firmly by the elbow. "No note of any kind was found."

As they walked out of the cubicle, Justin felt cold rush through him, starting in his stomach and working out toward his head and legs. His feet were so cold that he could hardly walk.

He was aware that the showroom was full of customers, single people and couples, clustered around the beautifully polished cars laid out here and there on the beautifully polished showroom floor. The buzz of conversation died as he walked across the floor, flanked by the two policemen, until there was no sound except the three sets of footsteps. In the terrible silence he could hear his own feet, shuffling slightly, and the squeak of the policemen's heavy shoes as they moved beside him. The front door, with the police car waiting just outside it, seemed very far away.

Next to it stood Mr. Manning, his face white with fury.

*   *   *

By the time the police had run out of different ways of asking him the same few basic questions about himself and each one of his classmates, it was too late for Justin to go back to work. He headed home. He felt desperately tired. More than anything else, he felt that his boring but peaceful little life had been completely turned on its ear.

It would be good to get home to Heather and the kids. Heather would have supper waiting, he thought while he trudged up the stairs toward their apartment. And then while she gave the children their baths, he'd snatch a peek at the sports page and see if his team still had a chance at the pennant, and then he'd read to Sarah and tuck her into bed. That's all he needed. Just a nice, quiet evening with his family. He loosened his tie, turned the key in the lock, and pushed the door open.

He'd forgotten about Hugo.

The living room was barred by a line of kitchen chairs marching across the rug. Beyond the chairs, the couch was awash in magazines and crumpled paper food wrappers. The curtains at one window were hanging crooked. At the other window, the curtains were completely gone.

What on earth was going on? "Hello?" Justin called. "Where is everyone?"

He stepped into the kitchen. In the middle of the floor stood a strange shape which he realized was the kitchen table draped in a sheet. From under the table came a murmur of voices punctuated by muffled giggles. There was no sign of Heather. And no sign of supper.

"Hello?" Justin called again.

"Papa?" Sarah's face, rosy with laughter, appeared under the edge of the sheet. "We're in a tent, Papa! We're camping! Do you want to come in too? We can make room!"

Justin bent down and lifted the corner of the sheet. Hugo was crunched up beside Sarah with his bony knees tucked up around his ears. His narrow chin was already scraggly with three days' growth of beard, and his hair stood out in wisps all over his head. His elbow poked out through a huge hole in the sleeve of his baggy purple sweater as he stirred something in a saucepan with a big wooden spoon.

"What are you cooking?" Justin asked, knowing that he didn't want to know.

"Fried worms in chocolate sauce!" Sarah squealed and fell over on her side laughing.

Hugo tipped the saucepan to reassure Justin that it was empty. "Maybe you'd rather it was beef stew?" he asked.

"Fried worms will be just fine," Justin said. "What's going on in the living room?"

"Oh, we didn't have a car so we took the train to get to our camping trip. Mama didn't come with us. She's in the bedroom lying down. She's got the baby with her. She said they were tired."

Never mind supper. Maybe he'd just lie down with Heather and the baby. But when Justin dropped the sheet and straightened up, he found Heather standing in the bedroom doorway and holding the baby, who was wriggling to get down and join the fun under the table. "Are you all right?" Justin asked.

Heather gave a tired shrug. "I'm with children all day long," she said and put the baby down on the floor. He immediately crawled over to the table and disappeared under the sheet, setting off another round of shrieks and giggles.

"Your boss phoned sometime this afternoon," Heather said. "He was on the answering machine. I guess Hugo was too *busy* to answer the phone. Anyway, Mr. Manning sounded all bent out of shape, asking if you were intending to come back to work or whether the police had decided to keep you." She looked up at Justin, and he could see that there were dark circles under her eyes. "What's going on, Justin?"

Justin told her about his afternoon at the police station. "I think they're figuring that Professor Quint was murdered, or at least that something happened to him that brought on a heart attack," he finished. "They're trying to work up a motive. They thought at first that they might have a robbery on their hands. But I guess they finally decided I wouldn't kill my professor for a calculator, even a fancy one, so they let me go."

"Well, Mr. Manning will never forgive you for getting hauled out of his showroom by the police in front of customers." Heather rubbed both hands over her face. "There was one other call for you on the answering machine. No message."

"Who was it?"

"Like I said, there was no message. It wasn't a voice I'd heard before. It sounded like he had a cold or something—he was talking in a kind of a whisper. He just said your name, waited for a moment, and then hung up."

"Well, if it was important, he'll call back," Justin said. "What's for supper?"

"Supper!" Heather snapped. "Who can make supper with *this* going on? He sits in here all day eating our food and leaving stuff around and playing games on your computer. Then when I get home, he gets the kids all wound up! I feel like a prisoner in my own home!"

"Ssh! He'll hear you!" Justin pulled Heather into the living room. He couldn't find a clear spot on the couch, so he drew her over to the line of kitchen chairs.

"Justin, you've got to talk to him!" Heather wailed. "He's your friend!"

"*My* friend!" Justin said. He dropped into the chair behind Heather's. He had begun to feel as if they really were on a train, but no one had told him where the train was headed. "He just used to live upstairs from me, that's all. He was always just *there*, a fact of life like four walls and a roof over your head." He paused, working up his courage. "Did you talk to Nellie?"

"How can I talk to Nellie?" Heather shouted. "Especially now that she's thinking of going to work for the competition? How can I tell her that her husband has turned into one of our children?"

*   *   *

Late that night, after supper was finally cooked and eaten and after the household finally quieted down, Justin lay awake, staring at the ceiling.

"Justin?" Heather's voice was hardly more than a rustling sound in the dark. "Justin, this business with Professor Quint, it's all over, isn't it? The police are done with you, right?"

"Come on, honey, think about it! I've got a good job— I've been at Manning's for more than six years! We have two cars. We pay our rent on time. If I'd wanted that calculator, I could've bought one. No, the police don't think I killed Quint. We're not going to get sucked back into this. Not a chance."

He hoped she believed it.

He wished he could.

CHAPTER 5

Friday afternoon, according to the newspaper, was the date set for Professor Quint's funeral.

Although he had hardly known the guy, Justin felt somehow that he'd better be there. He almost hoped Mr. Manning would refuse him the time off, but old Manning was a real soft touch when it came to things like small children and funerals.

Just before three o'clock, Justin had found a parking spot on the street alongside the grounds of City College and joined the small crowd of people entering the college's old brick chapel. Most of the people filing in to sit on the long wooden pews as the organ groaned above them had the same, slightly dusty look of the college itself—other college professors, Justin surmised. The front of the chapel was empty except for a half-dozen huge bouquets of flowers. Justin sat down and tried to mold himself to the hard wooden bench.

He spotted Rachel and Stacy sitting together near the front. Were the other members of his class there? Without moving his head, he slid his eyes to the left. Near the middle of the room hunched James Shaner, staring at the floor. Beyond him Fred Whittaker perched nervously on the edge of his bench, his head twitching in quick little movements like a bird's. He glanced toward Justin and immediately looked away.

On the other side of the aisle was Remington Trask, gnawing on his fingernails. Tucked under an open window was the man who sneezed. On the pretense of straightening his suit coat, Justin peeked around behind him and spotted a few other young men he thought looked familiar, one still in his Green Bay Packers sweatshirt. Everyone seemed to be there. All the people the police had questioned him about, over and over— they were all there.

He faced the front again and caught Rachel looking back at him. As he turned toward her, her eyes slid away, and she bent her head to say something to Stacy.

What had the police asked his classmates about *him*?

And what had his classmates said?

Questions and weird thoughts and more questions slammed around in his head. And one firm thought: murder. If the police were so interested, Quint *must* have been murdered.

Justin looked over again at Fred Whittaker, sitting there like a fat old owl. *What about Fred?* He had left before Justin did, the night that Quint was killed. Could he be the killer?

Or Rachel? She'd gone to ask Quint a question. That's what she'd *said*, anyway.

Justin shifted uncomfortably on the bench and tried to listen to the service. But all through the next hour, the thoughts bounced back and forth in his head like a game of handball played by a maniac.

At last the organ set up its groaning again, and the roomful of people stood up and started pressing themselves into the center aisle to file out toward the back of the chapel. Justin found himself pushed up elbow to elbow with James Shaner, but Shaner stared straight ahead without speaking. Just in front of them, Fred was jammed between two ladies who were maintaining a conversation in excited whispers over the top of his head. Justin tried to nod to Fred, but Fred kept his face turned away.

By the time Justin got out onto the front steps, the other members of his class had disappeared.

Feeling almost lightheaded, Justin paced slowly along a walkway that cut diagonally across the college grounds, heading in the direction of his car. The dull roar of rush-hour traffic pushing its way uptown filled his ears. He envied all those folks leading normal lives, hurrying home, feeling good about the approaching weekend. He wished he could just hop in his car and—

Suddenly he realized that the sound was coming from behind him.

He swung around. A car was rushing toward him down the walkway.

He leapt back. The car hurtled by in a surge of blue metallic light, so close that Justin could feel the heat of the engine. A sharp pain snatched at his elbow. He fell backward and slammed full-length against the grass.

He wasted a long moment trying to figure out why he was looking closely at small green leaves clustered along a twig. At last he understood that he was lying partly under a bush. But why? Then his addled brain began to move again and he remembered the car. The car! He scrambled to his feet and looked toward the street. The car had disappeared into the stream of traffic flowing by on the street.

Justin brushed himself off, hot with anger. The stupid fool! Driving on the walkway, not watching for pedestrians, going like a bat out of hell! Jail was too good a place for an idiot like that! If Justin's reflexes hadn't been so good, he could have been killed! What if it had been some old geezer walking along? City College could have lost another professor in the same week! Sputtering and fuming, Justin finished his journey to his car.

*   *   *

When he pushed open the door to his apartment, he could see Hugo in the far corner, hunched over the computer. "You should have seen what just nearly happened to me!" he called from the front hall as he checked his suit coat for grass stains before hanging it in the closet. "Some jerk was driving on the walkway at the college, and he almost ran me over!"

"Life in the big city," Hugo murmured. "You gotta be quick. Take *that*, alien monster!"

The computer screen flashed with strange shapes and sudden explosions. "What's that you're playing?" Justin asked.

"Alien Attack," Hugo said as the screen changed again to show a rocket, blasting across a desert landscape. "I'm up to Level 6 already. Darn! Now see what you've made me do!" The rocket disappeared in a shower of shimmering bits and pieces. "That was my last rocket too!"

"I didn't know my computer could play anything like that," Justin said.

"It couldn't. I've upgraded the memory and installed a new motherboard. You'll like it. I've put in some other— Darn! Didn't see that coming!" He jabbed at the computer mouse. "I'm dead for sure. Oh—you had a phone call a couple of hours ago."

"Who was it?"

"Didn't leave a name. Said you'd know who it was. Take *that*, alien monster!"

Justin stepped into the living room and looked around. The couch was clean for once, but Hugo's purple sweater was slung over the lamp with one sleeve dripping something into a widening damp spot on the rug. In its place, Hugo was wearing the blue wool sweater that had been Justin's Christmas gift from Heather.

"Uh, Hugo, that sweater you're wearing—Heather wouldn't like—" His voice trailed off.

A half-gallon carton of ice cream, open, with a spoon stuck into it, sat on the desk beside the computer. A thin stream of sticky white fluid wound from the corner of the box across the desk and under a pile of papers behind the computer.

"Hugo!" Justin gurgled. "The ice cream!"

"Huh? Oh, the ice cream!" As Hugo lunged for the carton, the spoon flipped out in a spray of melted ice cream and danced across the computer keyboard on its way to the floor. Holding the carton high above his head, Hugo raced for the kitchen, leaving a trail of gooey puddles across the rug.

They were still wiping the ice cream off the bills and paycheck stubs that had been stacked behind the computer when Heather came in with the children. She took in Hugo's sweater on the lamp, and Justin's sweater, now smeared with ice cream, on Hugo. She couldn't see what they were working on back there in the corner, but from the looks on their faces she knew she didn't want to know. "That's it!" she yelled. "Now! Justin, you're going to talk to Hugo *now*! Not tomorrow! Not after supper! *Now!*"

"Come on, Hugo," Justin said, scuttling past Heather, "let's go for a walk. I need to buy a newspaper." Hugo was right behind him.

"So, Hugo," Justin began, as they slouched away up the sidewalk, "what's with you and Nellie?"

"She threw me out," Hugo said. "She said I was sloppy. She said I can't keep a job." Hugo shrugged. "I don't understand what's the big deal. She knew all that when we got married."

Justin hid his grin by busying himself buying a newspaper from the newsstand on the corner. "Well, you were doing better for a while there," he said as they turned back toward home.

"Yeah, but I got tired of being someone else's renovation project. It's like this apartment building next door to yours." He jerked his head toward the building as they passed. "How long have they been fixing this up? What are they working on now, the roof?" He glanced up. *"Watch out!"* he screamed.

Hugo leapt into the air. His arm snaked out and hooked around Justin's neck. Justin flew forward, his arms flailing. The sidewalk was hurtling toward him. As it smashed into him, there was a rush of wind above him and a tremendous crash. Hugo's body thudded against his back, and the wind whooshed out of his lungs. Brakes squealed. Horns sounded. A woman's scream hung in the air.

Justin lay facedown on the sidewalk, dazed, choking. He tried to move, but Hugo's weight pinned him to the concrete. "Hugo—" he gasped. "For God's sake—"

"Hold on, guys!" someone shouted. "We're coming! Don't try to move!" Car doors slammed. Footsteps pounded along the sidewalk. "We'll get this off you! Are you all right? Somebody'd better call an ambulance!"

Justin was aware of feet and legs shuffling around him as their owners worked on something above him. "Careful! Careful!" a voice called. "Okay, all together now, on the count of three. One— Two— Three!"

The weight above Justin was suddenly less. He could breathe again. But Hugo refused to get off him.

A siren sounded in the distance, coming closer. "Help's coming. Don't move him—he's unconscious," a voice said just above Justin's head. "We could have a head injury here."

"I'm okay," Justin gasped. "I just had the wind knocked out of me, that's all."

A face suddenly appeared, turned sideways to line up with his. "You all right? The ambulance'll be here in a second. They'll get you and your buddy fixed up, and then everything'll be fine. You were lucky, man! I saw the whole thing! Your pal here saved your life!"

The siren wailed louder until the whole street reverberated with the sound and then suddenly fell silent. Doors slammed, footsteps hustled toward him. "What's the problem here?" an authoritative voice asked.

"This new section of wall fell from up there!" someone said. "It came right down on these guys. They were just about smashed right into the sidewalk!"

"This one's unconscious, but he seems to be breathing all right," another voice reported.

"Okay. Backboard. You get the straps. All set?" Hands worked quickly around them. A moment later, Hugo was carefully lifted away.

Justin pushed himself into a sitting position. "Easy there," someone said. "Let's check you over."

"What happened?" Justin asked. "Where's Hugo?"

"This whole section of the wall fell from up there," said a man with a small dog on a leash. "Your friend evidently took most of the blow."

"Yeah!" said a woman holding a bag of groceries against one hip. "I was on the other side of the street, and I just happened to look over. Your friend looked up, and he saw this stuff coming down, and he grabbed you out of the way and landed on top of you. It all happened so fast! One second it's a clear sidewalk, and the next second— wham! Stuff falling everywhere!"

"But where is he?" Justin asked again. "Where's Hugo?"

"He'll be at Central Hospital," the ambulance driver said. "How about you? Do you want to ride in and let a doctor check you out?"

"No, I'm fine." Justin struggled to stand on his wobbly legs. He felt like a new colt. "I live right here. My wife will be wondering—"

"We're off then." The ambulance driver disappeared. A moment later, the siren whooped and the ambulance pulled away.

Justin stood looking at the twisted mess of wood and masonry heaped around him on the sidewalk. The spot where he had been standing when Hugo grabbed him was completely covered with a good ton of debris. There was no question that Hugo had saved his life.

But what about Hugo?

He turned and staggered toward his own doorstep, leaving the onlookers still discussing the hows and whys of a large chunk of a building suddenly deciding to separate itself and drop four stories to the ground.

He climbed the familiar stairs to the familiar hallway, unlocked his door with his good old house key, and pushed the door open. Through the doorway, the living room was neat and clean. Heather was in the kitchen where she usually was at this hour, making supper. Casey was in his high chair, pursuing his favorite hobby of waving his arms and legs, while Sarah sat at the kitchen table, her new box of crayons open beside her, drawing a picture. It all looked so normal that Justin felt as if he had just stepped in from another planet.

"What was going on next door?" Heather asked. "I heard a siren, but I couldn't see anything out the window, and I couldn't leave the kids."

"Hi, Papa!" Sarah called before he could answer. She held up her picture. "I'm drawing this for Hugo."

"By the way, where *is* Hugo?" Heather asked, her voice somewhat muffled as she reached for something in the back of the refrigerator. "Did you actually get rid of him?"

"You're not going to believe this," Justin said.

CHAPTER 6

"Well, it'll be a quiet weekend anyway," Justin said.

Heather was down on her knees, trying to scrub the last of the ice cream out of the rug. "That's a heck of a way to get rid of a houseguest, sending him to the hospital."

"Are we going to go see Hugo now?" Sarah asked, jumping up from her favorite position stretched out with her head on her teddy bear in front of the Saturday morning cartoons. "I have to take him my picture!"

"I'm sorry, honey, they don't let little kids in the hospital. Now, don't cry—we'll be sure Hugo gets the picture."

Heather sat back on her heels with her head cocked to one side, scrutinizing the rug. "I guess that'll have to do. Let's just park the kids for a few minutes with Martha across the hall while we run down and see Hugo."

"No!" Justin's voice was so sharp that Heather

looked up at him, startled. "Let's take them over to Mrs. Grasso's place."

"But that's all the way across town!"

"It'll be nice for her," Justin said firmly. "Mrs. Grasso always says she doesn't see the kids often enough. Come on, Sarah, run and get a sweater or something, and get one for Casey too." Avoiding Heather's eyes, he rummaged in the closet for his own jacket.

He hadn't told her about the near-miss with the blue car on the walkway at City College yesterday afternoon. But when he put that together with the falling masonry on the sidewalk yesterday evening, he couldn't help seeing a pattern beginning to emerge. Someone was after him. And that someone knew where he lived. And that someone's aim was getting better. There was no way he was going to leave his kids where he couldn't keep an eye on things.

It took half the morning to get the kids ready, drag through traffic to Mrs. Grasso's house, answer Mrs. Grasso's million-and-one questions about every aspect of their lives, and then beat their way across town to the hospital. When they finally arrived in his room, Hugo was propped up in bed wearing a toothy grin, topped off by a large white bandage wrapped rakishly around his head. "Hey, guys!" he called as they appeared around the curtain that surrounded his bed, "how's everything at home?"

"Sarah sent you this." Justin held up her picture, which was now adorned with the words GET WEL QIK. "She says it's you." He stepped forward to hand Hugo the picture, then faltered as he realized that Nellie was sitting tucked into a corner of the curtain.

"Oh, hi, Nellie, I—" Heather's voice started and stalled like a car on a cold morning.

The corners of Nellie's mouth turned up a quarter of an inch in a miniature smile as she nodded at Heather, but she did not speak. Her silence seemed to reach out and cover them up, smother them. Neither Heather nor Justin could think of a thing to say.

Somewhere down the hall a loudspeaker summoned a doctor to the nurses' station.

Only Hugo seemed not to mind the quiet that was settling into the room. "She said it's me, did she?" he asked, examining the picture carefully. "That's my little princess."

"Nellie, did Hugo tell you that he saved Justin's life?" Heather said. "Seriously, Justin would have been killed if Hugo hadn't—"

"Yes, Hugo told me all about it," Nellie said. "Don't worry, I know that he is a hero." She reached out her small brown hand and smoothed the white bandage on Hugo's head. "I know what Hugo is," she said, "and what he is not."

"Well, I guess we've got to be going," Heather said. "Thanks so much for what you did, Hugo. See you on Monday, Nellie." Heather melted away beyond the curtain, and her shoes clacked on the linoleum as she made her escape into the hallway.

"Hugo, just one thing I've got to ask you," Justin said, clasping the footboard of Hugo's bed. "What did you see when you looked up?"

"I saw that chunk of wall coming at us," Hugo said. "What else?"

"That's exactly what I want to know! What else? Up on the roof— Did you see anyone—?"

From below the bandage, Hugo's eyes stared straight into Justin's. "I don't remember," was all he said.

*   *   *

The air in Mrs. Grasso's apartment was heavy with the aromas of good food: the rich, meaty smell of lasagna and the comforting, homey smell of bread baking. When Sarah opened the door for Justin and Heather, Mrs. Grasso was just sliding a cake pan into the oven, nudging it into place next to the huge, bubbling lasagna.

She straightened up and propped her hands on her ample hips. "Ah, there you are," she said. "You're staying for lunch, of course?"

Justin bent down to kiss her cheek, which felt papery-dry against his mouth—when had Mrs. Grasso become so old?—and gave her a hug for good measure.

From its cushion in the corner, the dog began to growl a tiny growl. "Now, Clarence, behave yourself!" Mrs. Grasso called. "I'm allowed to have a hug from a handsome gentleman now and then." The dog dropped its chin back into the cushion but kept up its muttering.

"Oh, Clarence," Sarah said, curling up on the cushion and putting her arms around the dog's neck, "what is it? Why are you growling all of a sudden? Papa, I think maybe Clarence doesn't like you!"

"That dog has never liked me," Justin said cheerfully. "I think it's because Mrs. Grasso named it after her husband." He gave Mrs. Grasso another hug and laughed as he realized his shirt was now well-dusted with flour.

He pulled out a chair at the tiny table and sat down, stretching out his long legs comfortably and gazing around the kitchen. He felt more at home here, he realized, than anyplace else in the world. The countertop cluttered with cookbooks and grocery store coupons, the refrigerator covered with photos of grandchildren, the gleaming pots hung overhead, ready to produce incredible meals, even the brown drums and bugles marching up the wallpaper, all said *home* to him. The house he had grown up in had been like that until his father took off, leaving his mother permanently sad. After that, he had never felt truly at home until he had first met Mrs. Grasso.

Heather seemed relaxed too. She settled into a chair opposite Justin and watched Casey watching the wall clock, which was in the shape of a cat with a tail and two huge eyes that moved back and forth to mark the passing seconds. Casey chortled and reached his pudgy little hands toward the swinging tail.

"And how's our Hugo?" Mrs. Grasso asked as she hustled plates, warm from the back of the stove, onto the table. "He'd better be well enough to eat—I've got another pan of lasagna for him waiting to go into the oven."

"If anything could make a person well," Heather said dreamily, "it would be a pan of your lasagna."

*   *   *

Their own apartment, when they returned to it, seemed empty and quiet. The afternoon stretched endlessly into evening and finally into night.

Sunday wasn't much better. Justin dug out his math homework and tried to work on the truth tables Professor Quint had assigned so long ago, while Heather listlessly turned the pages in a magazine. Even the children were subdued. Sarah sat at the kitchen table surrounded by her crayons, drawing another picture for Hugo just in case someone went to the hospital. Casey fell asleep in a small heap in the middle of the living room floor, his cheek pressed against the rug and his little rump in the air.

Then the doorbell rang.

It was Hugo in the same pants and pink high-top sneakers he'd been wearing on Friday, with Justin's blue wool Christmas sweater now shredded across one shoulder and somewhat shrunk from its trip through the hospital laundry. "I'm home!" he announced.

Justin simply stepped back from the door to let him in. "After all," he told Heather later, "you can't turn away a guy who's just saved your life."

Not that Sarah would have allowed him to send Hugo away. But neither, Justin suspected, would Heather.

*   *   *

"That building next door has been under renovation for months and months," Justin told Hugo as they lounged on the couch over a couple of beers while Heather and the kids whipped up some supper in the kitchen. "I've walked past it a million times without giving it a thought. But on Friday afternoon, if you hadn't happened to look up just at that instant, well, I'd be nothing more than a grease spot on the sidewalk right now."

He took a long drag on his beer. "The police said the construction workers should have been a lot more careful about securing it before they shut down for the weekend. But I still keep thinking about it: why did that hunk of wall pick that *particular* moment to fall—just as I walked under it? Somehow I don't think it was by chance."

"You think someone's after you? What about me? If you'll remember," Hugo laughed, fingering the bandage that still circled his head in a lopsided orbit, "I was there too."

"No, I think it was me that accident was meant for," Justin said, and he told Hugo about the blue car that had done its best to pick him off the walkway after the funeral.

Hugo whistled. "I see what you mean. You figure it's got something to do with that professor getting killed?"

Justin nodded. "That's got to be it."

They both upended their bottles and took long, philosophical swallows.

"Hey, Justin," Hugo said after a moment of silence, "remember that phone call?"

"What phone call?"

"Remember the other day I told you someone had called just before you got home? I picked up the phone and said hello, and this voice said, 'Justin Cobb,' real slow, like something out of a horror movie. Sort of whispering. When I said, 'No, this is Hugo,' he just hung up. Click. Conversation over." Hugo looked at Justin over the neck of his beer bottle. "That might have been your buddy—your blue-car-driving, wall-pushing buddy."

Justin's head snapped up. "Heather said something about a call on the answering machine! I wonder if it's still on the tape!" In two long strides he was across the living room. "Darn! Someone called for Heather yesterday morning and taped over it."

"Hey, man, cool it! I was just kidding." Hugo looked embarrassed at getting Justin so worked up. "It's natural to be upset. You've had a couple of close calls—it makes you think. But seriously, that doesn't mean someone's out to get you."

"I've got to think!" Justin re-crossed the living room and threw himself down on the couch. "You know, I got a phone call at work the day after Quint was killed. The receptionist told me about it just as the police arrived. Hey, maybe I've still got her note!" He catapulted off the couch, dashed to the hall closet, and pawed through his jackets until he found the suit coat he'd been wearing that day. He reached into the pocket. Penny Koch's little pink *while-you-were-out* slip was still there.

In the line where the caller's name should have gone, Penny had drawn a big question mark with a circle around it. In the message line, there were just four words: *Don't talk to them.*

Hugo peered at the slip over Justin's shoulder. "Don't talk to who?"

"The call came in just before the police arrived," Justin said.

Hugo, unable to restrain himself again, shook his head dramatically. "There you have it," he said. "The police arrived and you talked to them."

Justin dropped onto the couch again and pressed the beer bottle against his forehead. "I didn't have a whole lot of choice."

"Mmm," Hugo agreed.

"But this still doesn't answer the basic question: why *me*? Why does someone think *I* know something the police would be interested in? Wait!" Justin's eyes widened, and the hand holding the beer bottle sagged to his lap. "Oh, no. No!"

"What? What?" Hugo demanded.

"It must be that note! I shoved a note under Professor Quint's office door on Wednesday night to tell him I had his calculator. The police never found the note. Their answer was that I'd never written it."

Now, sitting on his own couch, listening to the happy evening sounds of his little family in the next room, Justin realized that there was another answer.

The killer had still been inside Quint's office when Justin knocked on the door.

That meant the killer had the note.

"What did I write in that note?" he begged Hugo. "I just told him I'd return the calculator the next day. Right? That's all I said, right?"

But as if it were laid out in the air in front of him, his eyes saw a slip of white paper with his hand marching across it—writing down his name, his phone number at work. His phone number at home.

He felt as if the couch he was sitting on had suddenly dropped right through the floor, to let him fall endlessly through empty space.

He couldn't go to the police. They didn't believe the note had ever existed.

He was on his own. It was just him—him and Heather and Sarah and the baby.

CHAPTER 7

Monday.

Sometimes Heather dreaded Mondays—the kids at the day care center worn-out from being allowed to stay up late during the weekend, Laurie rushing in a few minutes late and slamming the refrigerator door, another long week stretching endlessly ahead.

But this week she had been glad to see Monday come. Perhaps a new week would be a new beginning for her family. Last week had started with Justin starting college, continued by adding Hugo to their household, and ended with a funeral, a police investigation, and Hugo and Justin almost getting killed. She never wanted to go through another week like that one!

The day had gone smoothly at Little Friends. Nellie was her usual quiet self as she moved about the main room setting out the finger paints or helping the children pick up the blocks. The whole long day, right until she

64

left in the afternoon, she hadn't mentioned another word about James Shaner's plan for a day care center at City College. Heather would never say it out loud, but she sort of hoped Professor Quint's death had made everyone forget about renovating Eastman Hall at all.

The last parent finally showed up, pouring out a steady stream of apologies from the moment she scurried in through the red door to the moment she pushed her child out through it again. Heather was still in such a good mood that she managed not to point out that the woman had been late two or three times last week too. She gathered up Casey, supervised Sarah's job of putting out the lights in the main room and the kitchen, and pushed open the door to the alley.

She felt the man's presence before she saw him. He was standing at the end of the alley, holding something against his chest, a large dark shape against the brightness of the street beyond. He stared at her for a heartbeat, and then he was simply gone.

She backed in through the door and closed it and stood there in the darkened kitchen, panting. "What's the matter, Mama?" Sarah asked from behind her. "Why aren't we going home?"

"We'll go home in a few minutes, darling. I just need to check to make sure we have enough milk for tomorrow." She opened the refrigerator and elaborately counted the cartons of milk. "Yup," she said, peering out the window into the alley, "that looks like just the right amount of milk. We can go home now. Let's go!"

"Ow! Mama, you're squeezing my hand too tight!" Sarah wailed. "I can get in the car by myself! Don't push me!"

Heather leapt into the driver's seat and locked the car doors before turning around to buckle the children in. As she started the car, she resolved to talk to Justin. If this guy was hanging around the day care center, she had to do something about it. He might be after one of the kids— someone's estranged father, perhaps, looking to change the rules in a custody fight. They'd had trouble with that kind of thing before. Justin would know what to do.

But she was so late getting home that Justin had already left for class. She forgot to tell him about the man until several days later. When it was almost too late.

*   *   *

The nine students sat jittering under the humming florescent lights, waiting for class to start. They had all been early. They all faced front. No one spoke.

The question that hovered in each person's mind was so large, so obvious, that it might as well have been written in huge letters on the chalkboard: *Which one of us did it?*

The police were still working on it, Justin knew, because they'd been back this afternoon at Manning's Auto Sales to ask him more questions about why he had stayed behind after class last Wednesday and exactly when he had left. They asked him again and again about the note he alleged that he had written. If only he had never mentioned the note. If only he had never written it!

In the front row, Stacy whispered something to Rachel, and Justin realized that he was straining to hear. A rifle-shot sneeze blasted through the silence, and everyone jumped. "Sorry, sorry," the man by the window murmured into his handkerchief. Fred Whittaker patted his pencils back into place in his breast pocket. Remington Trask heaved his weight onto the other fleshy elbow and chewed at a fingernail; Justin noticed that he'd replaced the dog-eared notebook with a shiny new one which sported a soft-focus photograph of a covered bridge.

Justin glanced at his wristwatch: one minute past

seven. Maybe there wouldn't be a replacement professor after all. *You'd think the college would have called us*, he thought.

"Excuse me," said a hesitant voice from the doorway.

Chairs creaked as every face turned toward the back of the room. A young man in a conservatively cut business suit looked in at them, clutching the doorframe so hard that he was in danger of breaking off a chunk. His eyes looked overly large, almost bulbous, behind dark-framed glasses with thick lenses, like goldfish in a glass bowl. Between his smooth, plump, brown cheeks there was just barely room for a thin line of mustache above an apologetic smile. He couldn't have been more than twenty-four or twenty-five, Justin judged, even if he was wearing an expensive suit—not much older than the guys in the back row. Justin suddenly felt old.

"Is this Math 101?" the man asked. Several people nodded. *Who is this guy*, Justin wondered, *and why hasn't he heard about the invention of contact lenses? At least he doesn't look like another cop, come to interview the whole gang of us at once.*

"I'm Harry King," the man said, sliding one foot into the classroom as if half-expecting that it would be bitten off. "The college asked me to fill in for, um, Professor Quint, on account of, um, well, he's not exactly in a position to continue, if you know what I mean." The huge eyelids behind their glass coverings slammed together without making a sound. "Because he's dead. If you know what I mean," the man added and slid the other foot into the classroom. He still had not let go of the doorframe, so his body had begun to bend backwards like a blade of grass.

The first foot slid forward again, and now the man had to choose between letting go of the doorframe and falling over backwards. He managed to pry his fingers off the doorframe, then suddenly streaked for the front of the room, where he grabbed the edge of the teacher's desk and held on as if he were trying to keep it from getting away. "I'll just pick up where Professor Quint left off, if that's all right with all of you," he said. "We found Professor Quint's notes for this course in his office, and—" He released the desk, jammed his hand into an inner pocket of his suit coat, yanked out a packet of papers folded neatly lengthwise, and grabbed for the desk again. "Tonight we will be taking up probability."

"What's that?" squeaked Fred Whittaker.

"What happened to logic?" snorted James Shaner with a sneer that would have done credit to the late Professor Quint himself.

Harry King looked from one to the other, obviously unable to decide which question to answer first. He went with Fred's. "Probability is something that we all use every day. We say, 'What are the chances that I'll get a good job after college?' or 'The weather report says there's an eighty percent chance of rain today, so I'd better take an umbrella.' The science of probability was invented by a pair of French mathematicians about three hundred years ago to help some of their gambling buddies, but we use it for all sorts of things now. We use it heavily in industry and manufacturing, for example. Insurance companies use probability to figure out how much to charge you. You, ma'am," he said, suddenly pointing to Rachel in the front row, "you pay about half as much for car insurance as I do, or those gentlemen in the back row, because the insurance companies have worked it out that the probability of your having an accident is about half as great as it for us young male yahoos."

He grinned at the class, looking around to see if people were following his point. Justin was amazed how his nervousness had fallen away as he got into his topic—until Rachel snapped, "The probability of my having a car accident is zero, because I can't afford a car. I had to give it up after my young male yahoo husband stopped paying child support."

King's eyes swam toward her behind the thick lenses; his mouth moved, but no sound came out. His hands flapped in front of him, searching for the support of the desk. "Yes, well—" he croaked.

Justin felt bad to see the poor guy lapse back into this wretched nervousness. Besides, he'd just been starting to enjoy all this statistical stuff. It certainly seemed more like math than Professor Quint's obsession with logic. "You mentioned a moment ago that you use this probability in industry and manufacturing," Justin called out. "Can you tell us more about that?"

"Oh, yes!" the young man yelped in relief. "In my department, we work on quality control. We do random sampling of the product to check for defects of any kind. We use probability tables to tell us how many samples we have to take. See, we take a random sample and check it, and maybe this particular item is okay. But what are the chances that this one item is typical of all the rest? The probability tables tell us that."

King dug in his pants pocket and pulled out a coin. "It all begins with this," he announced and flipped it. Every head in the classroom moved in unison, watching the coin flash up into the air, hang suspended for a moment at the top of its parabola, then drop back neatly into his palm, and flip onto the smooth skin on the back of his hand. "Heads or tails?" he called to Justin.

"Uh—" Justin faltered, startled, "heads, I guess."

King examined the coin. "Nope. Tails." He looked up. "What were your chances?"

"Well, fifty-fifty, right?"

"Right. And what does that mean?"

"Um . . ." Justin thought for a moment. "That means in a hundred tries, it would come up heads fifty times and tails fifty times."

"Exactly!" King beamed. "In probability, you have the *law of large numbers*. That means you need a lot of examples, a *lot* of examples, to get the pattern. The more times you flip the coin, the more you'll see that it comes up heads exactly half the time. You could flip it ten times in a row and get heads—"

"That would mean the next flip would be more likely to be tails, just to even it out!" exclaimed Fred.

"No," laughed King, "on any one flip, the chances are still exactly fifty-fifty. My parents had seven boys. My mother really wanted a girl, and they just kept trying. She was getting kind of up there in age, but she figured she'd try once more. She convinced my father that with seven boys, it just *had* to be time for a girl. They didn't understand the laws of probability. Even with seven boys in a row, the chances were still fifty-fifty for the next one." He grinned. "They got me."

He turned to the chalkboard. "Here's another way of thinking of probabilities," he said, his voice slightly muffled by the fact that his back was turned, as he wrote the fraction $1/2$. "When you flip a coin, there are two ways it can land, heads or tails," he explained, tapping the *2*. And on each flip it can land only one way—that's the *1*. Now, in my family," he added, turning to face the classroom again, "with that many kids, there were all kinds of possibilities—three boys and four girls, four boys and three girls, and so on and so on. The chances of having eight boys in a row were only one out of sixty-four." He spun around and wrote $1/64$. "But still . . . when I was born, for my *particular* case, even with all those brothers, the chances of my being a boy were *still* one out of two. Surprise, Mom!" he shouted, throwing his plump hands up in the air. The chalk shot out of his fingers and shattered against the chalkboard behind him. "Sorry about that," he murmured. He looked up and down the length of the chalk tray. "I guess City College doesn't allow more than one piece of chalk per instructor. That'll teach me to restrain my enthusiasm!"

He faced the class again, dusting off his fingers, which set off the usual sneeze over on the window side of the room. "Let's do birthdays!" King urged. "I was born on May fifteenth. You, there!" He pointed again at Justin, whom he seemed to recognize as his major ally in the room. "How about you? When is your birthday?"

Justin wondered if this math class was going to jump from logic to probability and now to astrological signs, but he played along. "February fifth," he called out.

King went around the room, collecting birthdays. The dates seemed to be suitably random—several summer birthdays, a few more in winter, one in spring—until King came to Remington Trask. "February fifth," Trask whispered.

"Wow!" Fred gasped. He turned to Justin, and Justin could almost hear the wheels turning in his head. "That's the same as yours!"

"Amazing, right?" King crowed. "Actually, it's not all that amazing. There is only a limited number of dates that people can fit their birthdays into—365 of them. Out of any ten people, the probabilities are actually one in ten that two of them will have the same birthday. The probabilities rise, of course, the more people there are— out of fifty people, it's almost a sure bet. The odds were against us here, but not that badly. And we got lucky!"

Justin glanced over at Trask and found the fried-egg eyes staring fixedly at him. He sort of wished his mother had waited another day.

King bounced along onto the next topic, laying out a book, a chalkboard eraser, and a ballpoint pen on the teacher's desk and showing them how to figure out the odds of picking out the items in different combinations. He increased the number of items, showing how that raised the odds dramatically with each added item, and he was just demonstrating that the number of combinations possible with a 52-card deck churned out a number that ran to sixty-eight digits, when the someone in the back row called out, "Don't we get a break tonight?"

It was the young man in the Green Bay Packers sweatshirt—*a real fan or does he just happen to like that sweatshirt?* Justin wondered—and he looked dizzy. "I could really use a cigarette to help me think about all this," he apologized.

"Oh, sure, I'm sorry," King said. "Go ahead." But the entire back row was already out the door.

The rest of the class followed at a more leisurely pace. Justin would rather have stayed to talk to King, but somehow he felt the need to keep an eye on his classmates. He didn't feel as if he could afford to miss anything in the gossip department. Besides, ever since the police had been back to talk to him, he was dying to know if they'd talked to the others too.

The weather had turned cooler, as September often does, and the group was huddled around the relative warmth of the front entryway of the building. Everyone was there, even Trask, although only a few lit up cigarettes. They all eyed each other in uncomfortable silence.

"Well," said Justin in an effort to get things going, "this Harry King and his probability are certainly more fun than old Quint's logic."

Rachel whirled around to face him, eyes blazing. "How dare you say anything against poor Professor Quint? The poor man is killed, and you stand there *laughing* about it!"

"I didn't mean—" Justin stammered.

"You were here that night, the night he was killed, just hanging around, pretending to play with his special calculator. I saw you waiting for everyone else to leave. The police keep coming to the restaurant where I work, asking me questions about you. They think you know something you're not telling. Maybe they even suspect that you did it! But I'm telling you, *Mr.* Cobb, even if that restaurant job is nothing great, I have a child to support and I can't afford to lose my job over *you*! So I sure hope that if you do know something about Professor Quint's death, you'll go ahead and tell the police—and soon!"

"But I—"

"And another thing!" Rachel snapped. "I'm not at all sure that I want my little boy in a place run by anyone who would marry the likes of *you*!" She jerked her body around to look up at James Shaner, who was leaning his thin shoulder against the peeling paint of the doorframe. "I was reading in the newspaper about a student group getting the college to start up a new day care center," she said. "How soon do you think you can get it going?"

Shaner's narrow face was in shadow, but his earrings gleamed in the light from the hallway. "We're working on it. Pretty soon, I'd say."

Triumphantly, Rachel turned back toward Justin. "Just as soon as I find another place for Allen, the Little Friends Day Care will be minus one kid!"

"Hey, Rachel, that's not fair!" Justin sputtered. "I mean, the police have been talking to *all* of us, right?" He looked around the circle for support. "Right?"

The faces of his classmates were carefully blank. No one spoke.

Beside him, Trask was chewing on his fingernail. The fried-egg eyes shone palely in the dim light.

*   *   *

As they got ready for bed that night, Justin hardly heard Heather telling him about the man in the alley. Nothing had happened, after all, and he didn't want to get any conversations going about the day care center— not tonight, not until he'd had a chance to think of what to say to calm Rachel Hylen down. He snapped off the light, yanked the covers up over his shoulders, and butted his head deep into the pillow. He thought he wouldn't sleep, but he was instantly gone.

Heather nestled against him, reassured. If Justin didn't think there was anything to worry about, well, he was probably right. She let her mind drift, thinking about the new rug she wanted for the main room at the day care center and reminding herself to call tomorrow to make an appointment for Sarah's first visit to the dentist. She laid her arm across Justin's waist and pressed her forehead gently against the back of his neck. She sighed and let herself go down, down into the peaceful darkness.

Out in the living room a few hours later, hunched over the computer and his eighty-seventh game of Alien Attack, it was Hugo who first smelled the smoke.

CHAPTER 8

"Justin! Heather! Wake up!" Hugo stood over them, shaking them so hard that their bodies flopped in their bed like newly caught fish in the bottom of a boat. "Wake up! We're on fire!"

"What—?" Justin croaked, struggling upward out of sleep. But Heather was already on her feet, bolting for the door. "Fire?" she screeched. "Where? Justin, help me get the kids!" She dashed across the tiny hallway and snatched open the door to the children's bedroom.

Justin stumbled out behind her into the thick smoke which roiled toward them from the living room and almost instantly filled the hallway. "Oh, my God!" he shouted. "What's happening?"

Heather scooped the baby out of his crib and grabbed Sarah up in the other arm. "Call the fire department! Quick!" she shouted at Justin. The smoke burned her eyes, filled her throat, and left her coughing and gasping for breath. Mewling like a newborn kitten, Casey struggled in her arm, fighting for air, and she had to grapple to keep her grip on him without dropping Sarah.

"Never mind the fire department! We've got to get out of here! Come on—we've got to get the window open and get out onto that fire escape!" Justin started to feel his way through the smoke in the living room.

"Justin!" Heather shrieked. "Where are you? I can't see you!"

"This way!" Hugo called to them out of the smoke. "Get the children out! I'll go get the neighbors up! We don't have much time!" She could hear the door opening and his voice echoing in the corridor: "Fire! Fire! Get up, everybody!"

Heather felt completely disoriented, as though she were trying to find her way through a totally unfamiliar place in pitch darkness. The living room seemed vast. She wasn't at all sure which way it was to the window that opened out onto the fire escape. She tried to remember where Hugo's voice had come from. If they could find the door, they could work their way sideways to the window. And all this time her lungs burned and her rib cage heaved as if her body were refusing to take in the smoke. Her head prickled with tiny needles of pain—her lungs wanted to break open in her chest— Air—They needed air—

"Justin!" Heather gasped, and suddenly he was there, his tall, lean body at her elbow, reassuring just by its presence. "Which way—?"

"This way, I think—I'm not sure—" Suddenly Justin swayed and almost fell. Panic clawed at Heather's insides. *If he goes down, what will we do? We'll all die—We've got to think, got to figure it out—*

Justin grasped the back of a chair and hacked

desperately. "This way," he croaked. "Follow me." He took Casey from her and led the way, choking and wheezing, into the billowing smoke. Heather felt the panic rising in her again as he disappeared from her sight. *What if we're wrong? What if we're going the wrong way? How long do we have before we die of smoke inhalation?*

"Crawl under the smoke, Mama," said Sarah's calm voice in her ear. "That's what Officer Friendly said when he came to our school. Crawl under the smoke."

Heather paused for an instant, then dropped to her knees and hunkered low, Sarah still clamped in her arms. Yes, there was air here—wonderful, cool, sweet oxygen. It filled her burning lungs, spread out through her wracked body, chased away the splinters of glass slicing her brain. "Justin," she called, "get down! Get down and breathe!"

There was no answer. Justin and Casey were gone somewhere in the blackness of the living room. There was nothing but the churning smoke.

"Justin! Where are you?" She tried to crawl forward, hampered by Sarah's warm little body.

"I can crawl, Mama!" Sarah wrenched free and scuttled past the chair and on into the living room, under the thick layers of smoke that writhed like an evil blanket come to life and bent on killing those it covered.

"Stay with me!" Heather barked. She caught up with Sarah and crawled forward with Sarah's compact body between her arms. They made their way alongside the couch, around the end table, and toward the desk where the computer screen still glowed faintly through the smoke. That meant the window with the fire escape lay just ahead. But where were Justin and Casey? "Justin!" she called. "Justin, where are you?"

As if in answer, a siren screamed in the distance, coming closer. Out on the street, she realized, a jumble of voices shouted, "Fire! Fire! Help! Oh, help!" They seemed very far away, as if they had nothing to do with her. Inside the apartment, everything seemed muffled, as if she and her family and all their belongings had been packed for shipping in soft wrappings—thick, strangling wrappings—

Desperately she shook her head, which only set it to whirling. Little prickles of darkness danced behind her eyes. *We're running out of time—all of us,* she thought.

She pressed her cheek against Sarah's wiry back and forced her ribs to take in a deep breath. Then she grasped the windowsill to pull herself up and ran her hand up over the smooth glass, feeling for the lock on the top of the first sash. She twisted open the metal catch, then grappled with the heavy window, trying to force it up. *Oh, come on, come on.* With a rending shriek, it moved upward a few inches. She pressed her face to the space and sipped in one breath of the sweet, cool air of the outside world, then jammed her hands into the gap, wrapped her fingers around the sash, and yanked upward. A few more inches, then a few more, almost a foot . . .

"Sarah, come here!" she panted. She grabbed Sarah's little nightgown-clad body and pushed her through the gap. Her nightgown gleaming palely in the lights from the street, Sarah crouched like a little monkey on the metal rungs of the fire escape. "Stay there!" Heather hissed at her. "I've got to find Daddy."

She turned and faced into the living room again. There was nothing but smoke, thick, black, choking smoke packed solidly into every inch of space. "Justin!" she wheezed. Even to herself, her voice was a tiny sound in the smoke, lost amid the shouts and sirens and screams and horns that blared up from below as if a full-fledged war had suddenly broken out on their unimportant little side street, normally so quiet in the dead of night. This must all be a nightmare. Soon she would wake up and hear Justin breathing peacefully beside her. If she could only wake up! "Justin! Justin, where are you?"

And then there was a tiny little sound, a soft, sad little whimper. The sound entered into her through her heart rather than through her ears. It was Casey.

She dropped to her knees and crawled toward the sound. The room was so full of smoke now that even close to the floor there was very little air. She had to press her face almost to the rug to snatch a breath and then another one. She crawled past the legs of the desk, then to the back of the couch. "Casey!" she called. "Oh, Casey, where are you? Mama's here. Please, Casey!"

The whimper came again, close, close—but where?

She slithered along the length of the couch, sliding her shoulder along the fronts of the cushions to be sure of where she was, and around the far end. She stopped, listening, listening for that one tiny sound among the millions of sounds that crashed in around her from the street. *Oh, Casey, breathe. Breathe for Mama, and cry! Casey—*

The whimper came again, inches from her elbow. She reached out. A tiny, warm hand touched hers, and miniature fingers wrapped themselves around her thumb. "Oh, Casey!" She grasped him by the front of his pajamas and pulled him to her across the rug. He didn't resist but lay limply in the crook of her arm, too weak even to produce again that tiny, pathetic whimper.

She was down to seconds now, she knew that. She had to find Justin.

Dragging Casey with her, she pushed herself out away from the couch, keeping one bare foot pressed against its leg to keep from getting lost, and reached out across the rug. She swung her arm in wider and wider arcs, searching. Casey couldn't have gone far, could he, from Justin's body?

And then there he was, crumpled on the rug just a few feet from the couch. Quickly Heather bent her face to his. Was he still breathing? She couldn't tell. She pressed her ear against his chest and heard a faint flutter of heartbeat—or was it just the clatter of feet on the fire escape below the window? She couldn't tell, she couldn't tell. *Justin*, she told him, *you breathe, and I'll get us out. Is that a deal?*

She locked her fingers into the front of his pajamas and tried to drag him toward her, but his long, lanky body seemed to be attached to the floor. She'd always liked his being so tall, she thought, but now she wished she'd married a little guy. *I'm losing it*, she realized. *I'm going crazy, right here in the middle of my own living room rug! I've got to do this! I've got to get him out!*

She sat up into the smoke, bracing her heels against the rug, grabbed him under the arm, and pulled. But his arm flopped loosely, and the rest of him did not budge. Casey struggled weakly against her in her other arm.

This wasn't working. She couldn't move him with one hand. But if she left him while she took Casey to the window, she wouldn't be able to find him again. And it would be too late. *Think! Think, woman!*

Suddenly she visualized Justin the way he had held Casey when the baby had that ear infection that kept him up all night. Justin would lie sprawled on his back on the rug, watching television, with Casey draped across his chest. That position always seemed to soothe Casey, face down, ear to heartbeat. Now, gently, as if she were putting him down for a nap, she lay Casey across Justin's chest. Then she took a long breath of air from the last thin layer above the floor, grabbed Justin's pajamas by both sides of his collar, and began to pull. Inch by inch, his body slid toward her across the floor.

The couch seemed endless as she scrabbled along its length, digging her bare toes into the rug for purchase, pulling, pulling, checking to be sure Justin's passenger was still with them, pulling some more. She asked herself irrationally why they had ever bought such a big couch— if they'd got a smaller one, they'd be at the window by now. She counted the cushions as she worked her way by them, one, two, three, and then the other arm of the couch. Her hands cramped painfully, and the fabric of Justin's pajamas seemed to be ripping her fingernails right out of her fingertips, but still she pulled. Past the legs of the desk, wheezing, lungs burning, choking, until she had to take an instant to dip her face to the rug for more air. Now she could feel the air from the window. "Mama?" Sarah called.

"Coming, darling," she gasped. Her shoulder bumped the wall. She was there!

But how was she going to lift Justin over the sill?

She wrapped her fingers around Casey's round little tummy and raised him toward the window. "Sarah, honey, take Casey, please," she said, and suddenly Casey's weight lifted itself away from her hands. Then she straddled Justin's body, grabbed him under the arms, and heaved him upward. His head bobbled on the end of his neck, and he slumped back onto the floor. Her arms were so tired that the muscles jumped, but she tried again. And again. It was no use. She couldn't even lift his head toward the life-giving air.

"Mama, you and Daddy come out here now please," Sarah called. "Casey's all wobbly and he won't sit up."

Heather started up in panic. "Don't let go of him!" she shrieked. She felt as if she were split in a million pieces—

her children were out there by themselves, clinging to a fire escape three stories up on the outside of a burning building, and little Casey needed medical attention *now*, right this *instant*—but she couldn't leave Justin! If only Hugo hadn't been so quick to run off!

Below them the street was a forest of screams and shouts with the distant sirens winding through them like a river. Help was coming, but not fast enough, not fast enough. The fire escape clanged and bonged as footsteps rattled against it somewhere beneath them. People everywhere and no one to help them, no one to help!

Suddenly Sarah tipped so close to the edge of the metal platform, Casey still held close in her arms like a huge doll, that her face slid under the railing and hung right over the edge. "Sarah, be careful!" Heather screamed. "Sit up! Hold onto the railing!"

But Sarah was calling to someone far below. Her thin little voice was hardly more than a wisp of breeze amid the chaos of sounds in the surrounding streets. How could anyone hear her?

Someone did. The fire escape clanged with footsteps charging purposefully upward. Heather strained to see through the smoke that billowed past her face as it escaped out the partly open window. A head capped with wild-man hair and a pair of skinny shoulders appeared in the ladder gap in the fire-escape platform. Even before the head swiveled around to reveal the face, Heather knew that it was Hugo. Their Hugo, their beautiful Hugo.

He grasped the platform in both hands and jerked himself up next to Sarah in one lithe motion. In the next instant his arms were around the children. "Are you all right? Where're your parents?" he demanded.

"Hugo! Help me!" Heather called. "Justin's

unconscious—we've got to get him out!"

As fast as thought, Hugo was on his feet again. Crouching down, he wrapped his long fingers around the sash and jerked the window open all the way. He reached in, grabbed Justin under the arms, and yanked him up and out so quickly that Heather hardly had time to wrestle Justin's legs up over the windowsill before his body had disappeared outside, drawing her scrambling out after it.

"Bring the kids!" Hugo barked. He slung Justin's limp body over his shoulder and started down the ladder to the next platform. Heather scooped up Casey, and she and Sarah followed him down, down, into the riot of shouts and sirens on the street below.

The ambulance had just whooped in for a landing when they reached the street, and moments later Casey and Justin were loaded in, oxygen masks clamped over their faces. Heather and Sarah were lifted in to perch precariously on the edge of the bunks while the ambulance rocketed through the city streets. The familiar storefronts looked unreal to Heather as the lighted box on wheels containing everything she loved in the world lurched and swayed on its way to the hospital.

In the emergency room, Heather cuddled an exhausted Sarah in her arms while teams of men and women in apple green scrub suits worked around her husband and son. She wondered dully if her apartment building was busy burning to the ground out there in the nighttime city. She turned her gaze toward the window, looking for an extra-bright glow above the nearer rooftops. But she found that she didn't really care. All she wanted was for her husband and her baby to breathe on their own again and be well.

Hours later, everything seemed right with the world

again. Justin was awake and apologetic for losing his way in his own living room. Casey was fussing like his usual cranky self and squirming to rid himself of the nebulizer that was opening his lungs and filling his bloodstream once more with life-giving oxygen. Heather and Sarah had been allowed showers in the adjoining bathroom—Heather was astounded at the filth that swirled off them and down the drain—and Sarah was sleeping peacefully at the end of Casey's bed. Hugo had stopped in to report that the fire appeared to have been put out before it had a chance to do much damage to the building. Heather had thanked, and thanked, and thanked him for the fact that his ears had been tuned earlier to Sarah's tiny cry for help.

And then, near morning, two policemen arrived. They asked to speak to Heather alone.

"I'm Officer Mosher, Mrs. Cobb," said the older one, bowed with the strain of being up all night. "We've found where the fire started in your building. It began in a pile of rags—old towels, mostly—soaked in gasoline and placed in the corridor near your apartment door."

"A pile of towels?" Heather repeated numbly.

"Mrs. Cobb," the younger policeman cut in before she could ask how towels soaked in gasoline could possibly have found their way to the apartment building's upper corridor, "does your apartment have a smoke detector?"

"Well, yes, of course—"

"Did it go off? Is that how you escaped the fire?"

"No, I don't think so. Our friend Hugo was the one who woke us up. The smoke detector—oh, I remember. It needed new batteries and my husband was going to get some, but I guess he forgot."

The two policemen glanced knowingly at each other,

and Heather felt her stomach clench into a knot. She didn't like where this was going.

"Mrs. Cobb," Officer Mosher said, his voice sad, "we've been talking to your husband. We've also talked to other people who know him at City College and at his place of employment. I think you would have to agree that he has been acting very strangely lately."

"Mrs. Cobb," the younger policeman said brusquely, "we think your husband may have deliberately set this fire."

CHAPTER
9

In the morning, the fire
department announced that it was safe for the residents
of the apartment building to go back inside and try to
pick up their lives again where they had left off.

Heather got the news at the hospital where Justin was
dozing comfortably in his room with Casey tucked into a
crib right beside his bed. Heather left them in each
other's care, and she and Sarah took the bus home.
Official-looking cars were still parked out front while
various sorts of inspectors finished checking the building,
but otherwise the street looked weirdly normal as
Heather and Sarah walked toward the familiar front steps.

The apartment, on the other hand, looked dirty—and
oh, the *smell!* Even though the choking smoke of last
night was completely gone, the smell lingered everywhere:
in their clothes, the curtains, the bedclothes, the food in
the kitchen. Even the bare walls seemed to smell of
smoke. Heather opened the windows wide to the sweet

September morning, but she knew that wouldn't do it. Everything, *everything*, would have to be cleaned.

She phoned the day care center to make sure that Nellie was still managing all right with Laurie's help. Then she threw herself into a kitchen chair, propped her chin on her hands, and gave herself a few minutes to think about her interview with the police.

Of *course* Justin hadn't set that fire, she had told them. Justin wouldn't *do* a thing like that! Besides, ever since she'd had the kids, she'd become a really light sleeper, and she would have known in a moment if Justin had got up and gone out into the hallway with a pile of old towels.

And all of their towels were still in the linen closet, reeking of smoke but still stacked neatly just where she had put them. She'd checked.

It's bad enough having your husband and your son in the hospital and everything you own maybe ruined forever with the smoke, Heather thought, *without the police coming along and asking ridiculous questions!*

The front-door buzzer sounded, and Sarah leapt up from the thicket of crayons on the living room floor where she'd been making a GET WEL QIK card for her father. "Hugo!" she squealed at the tinny voice that responded to her questioning, and she pressed the button to let him into the downstairs hallway.

Heather watched her dance on tiptoes to the apartment door, waiting expectantly for Hugo's usual cheery *shave-and-a-haircut* knock. Hugo—what had *Hugo* been up to last night?

It had taken Heather more than a week to get used to Hugo's moving about in the living room after she'd gone to bed. But she'd learned to sort out the Hugo sounds, to classify them in her brain along with the noise of cars passing in the street and voices from other apartments, as sounds that she didn't need to attend to, so she could listen only for disturbances in the soft breathing from the other room or tiny voices calling "Mama!" She didn't even hear Hugo anymore. She knew she wouldn't have noticed him going out into the hallway and coming back in.

It had been Hugo who first smelled the smoke and waked them, then ran to wake the other residents. He had been a hero again as he had been when he saved Justin from the falling debris last week. Or—could he have set the fire in the first place? Perhaps he'd come to *like* being a hero, and he'd found a way of getting a little more excitement going—

Don't be silly, Heather told herself as Hugo popped through the door and swept the waiting Sarah into his skinny arms. *Don't even think like that. Hugo would never do a thing like that. For one thing, he's never made a plan in his life!*

Still, she had a hard time meeting his eyes when he bounded into the kitchen to ask after Justin and Casey. His hair, frizzy from recent shampooing, looked as if it were crackling with electricity. The blue jeans he wore looked surprisingly new, until Heather recognized them as Justin's, but the purple *Been There, Done That* sweatshirt was pure Hugo.

Been where? Done what? Heather wondered. She found herself staring down at the familiar wrecks that had once been high-top sneakers, now more black with soot than pink, as she told him, "Justin and Casey are going to be fine."

*   *   *

When Heather went back to the hospital around lunchtime, she found Casey kicking his bare toes against the bars of his crib while Justin sat propped up against several pillows writing on a sheet of paper laid out on his lap table.

Heather darted toward the crib. "Oh, look, Casey, they've taken that nasty nebulizer mask off of you!" she cried. He raised his chubby arms to her, and she scooped him out of the crib and held him close. Justin looked up and smiled, then bent over the lap table again. "What have you got there?" Heather asked, craning around him to see what he was doing. "Are you drawing designs for your dream car again?"

"No, I'm working on my homework for my math class," Justin said. "I'm checking out what the new instructor was telling us about probability." A coin flashed in a small arc above the table before Justin snatched it out of the air and slapped it against his wrist. "Heads or tails?"

"Um, heads, I guess," Heather said.

Justin lifted his hand and examined the coin. "Heads it is," he announced and made a mark on the sheet of paper.

Heather could see that the top third of the paper was covered with neat rows of hatch marks under the two headings *heads* and *tails*. There seemed to be a few more hatch marks under the *tails* side, but they were pretty even.

"I'm demonstrating the law of large numbers," Justin told her. "The more times I flip the coin, the closer it comes out to exactly fifty-fifty. When I first started, I had quite a run of heads, but it evened itself out after a while." The coin popped up, turning in the air, then dropped onto the table, circled itself for an instant like a basketball around the rim of the hoop, and flopped over on its side. Justin peered at it carefully. "Heads again," he said and made another mark on the paper.

"Well, I spent the morning in the apartment," Heather told him. "We've got a terrible cleaning job ahead of us.

I've already dropped your suits off at the dry cleaners, so you'll have something to wear to work when you get out of here. By the way, Mr. Manning wasn't happy at all when I called him. I told him you were in the *hospital*, for crying out loud, because your building was on fire and you almost *died*, and he acted as if that was no excuse for missing work!"

"Mmm," Justin said, and flipped the coin. "Tails." He made another hatch mark.

"Justin, are you listening to me? I'm trying to tell you—"

Justin looked up at her with a startled crook to his eyebrows, as if she had just walked into the room. "Where's Sarah?" he asked.

"I left her with Martha across the hall."

"Where's Hugo? Didn't he come home?"

"Oh, yes, he's there, but I—well, Martha hasn't seen Sarah in a while, and I didn't want to put Hugo to all the bother of looking after her, and—"

"Sarah's not a bother to Hugo. He adores her."

"I know. But." Heather let it drop. She couldn't explain to Justin the sudden uneasiness she felt about Hugo. Justin wasn't listening anyway. He was recording another flip of his coin.

"Well, since you're so busy," she said, "I'll go see if they'll let me take Casey home, and I'll go back and do some more cleaning—"

"No!" Justin was staring up at her, his eyes so wide that the whites showed all the way around the pupils. "Don't do that!"

"Don't what?" Heather asked, startled at the sudden change in him. "Don't clean? But—"

"Don't take the kids home! Go to Mrs. Grasso's place.

Now! Do this for me, Heather, *please*! At least until I get out of the hospital." Justin's face and neck were taut with strain. "Will you do it? Please? Will you?"

"Well, yes," Heather said slowly, "if it's that important to you."

"It is." Justin's firestorm of panic passed as quickly as it had come. The coin flashed. "Heads again."

"I'll get going, then," Heather said. But Justin didn't even look up as she carried Casey out of the room.

From the doorway she looked back at him, where he sat hunched over his sheet of paper. Maybe the police were right: maybe he *was* acting strange.

Not dangerous, of course, Heather assured herself, *but definitely strange.*

*   *   *

When Mrs. Grasso heard about the fire in their apartment building, she didn't give Heather a chance to express Justin's request. "You just pack up a few clothes for the little ones," she wheezed cheerfully into the telephone, "and you move right in here until Justin gets home from the hospital *and* your apartment is cleaned as good as new. Don't worry about a thing—there's plenty of room. When my grandchildren come, we get along in this apartment just fine. I'll put the coffeepot on, and you come right over and tell me all about it."

It felt so good to talk to someone, Heather thought, sitting in Mrs. Grasso's cramped and homey kitchen. Of course Mrs. Grasso's coffee was so weak that Heather could see right down to the bottom of the cup, but the plateful of warm sticky buns in the middle of the table sent up an aroma that made her feel that everything might possibly be all right after all. She couldn't face the day care center right now, with all the demands it put on her minute by minute all day long—and Laurie had promised to stay for the afternoon to help Nellie. No, what Heather needed right now was to be right here in this kitchen with this wise old lady.

"Justin's been acting so strange ever since he woke up in the hospital this morning," she told Mrs. Grasso. "He started counting up the heads and tails when he flips a coin, and he won't stop! He's filled in most of a sheet of paper with these little marks, and he just keeps going!"

Mrs. Grasso waddled over to the table, carrying a chipped china sugar bowl and a can of condensed milk. "Well, he's had a tough couple of days," she said, surveying the table to see if anything was missing. "Do you think the sticky buns will be enough, or do you need a little soup or something? How about the kids? I could fix them some soup, or maybe a little sandwich—"

"No, no, they're fine!" Heather leaned back in her chair so that she could see through the doorway into Mrs. Grasso's bedroom. The tiny room was almost entirely taken up by the big brass bed and a battered mahogany bureau, its walls so completely covered with framed needlepoint pictures of flowers that it was impossible to see the pattern of the faded wallpaper. In the middle of the bed, snuggled into a handmade quilt, Casey was deep into his afternoon nap. Sarah, who had been playing quietly with the dog, was spraddled across the narrow strip of rug in front of the bureau, sound asleep, with the dog curled against her, nose tucked under tail. Heather laughed. "No one's hungry in there! Everyone's zonked right out!"

Mrs. Grasso sighed, defeated, and sat down at the little table across from Heather. She poured milk into her coffee until the mixture was a pale brown, then lifted the cup to her mouth. Instead of taking a sip, she sighed again. "My Clarence acted a bit strange now and then," she said. "My husband, I mean. Not the dog."

Heather took another bite of sticky bun and waited.

"He collected things," Mrs. Grasso explained. "He started by collecting the usual things—stamps, coins, baseball cards. Then he expanded into all sorts of other collections. He had a dozen albums full of nothing but funny headlines he clipped from the newspapers. You know, like *Man Bites Dog*, or *Fire Chief Axed*. His favorite of all time was *Put Something Here*. He could never figure out if they meant it as a headline or had just forgotten to write one."

Heather smiled around the mouthful of sticky bun. "Sounds like fun," she said.

"Well, yes, except after a while he didn't seem to care about anything else! He'd buy four or five newspapers every day and go through them, just looking at the headlines. Then when he got tired of headlines, it was pigeon feathers. He'd walk down the sidewalk all hunched over, watching for feathers. He'd stick them down on sheets of paper, all carefully graded by size and color, and label them by date and location." Mrs. Grasso wrinkled her nose and took a gulp of coffee. "Pigeons are dirty," she added.

"For a while it was zebras," she went on. "Pictures of zebras. Books about zebras. Newspaper articles about zebras. We had bedsheets with zebras on them, and coffee mugs, and calendars, and even a living room rug with a couple of zebras and a lion. I always wondered about the rug. If he liked zebras so much, why would he want cover his floor with zebras that are about to become a lion's supper?"

Heather laughed in spite of herself. "That's a man for you, I guess."

Mrs. Grasso humphed into her coffee. "In the end, it was a collection that killed him. At least that's what I've always suspected. At that point he was collecting interesting license plate numbers. He'd write them down in a little book he always kept in his coat pocket. When the police found him, he had the book in one hand and a pen in the other."

"But how did that *kill* him?"

"He was driving our car at the time. I figure he saw a license plate number that was so interesting that he completely forgot he had a steering wheel in front of him, not a writing table! I've always wondered—" Her voice faded away.

"Wondered what?" Heather prompted.

"What the number was, of course!" Mrs. Grasso examined the plate of sticky buns, selected one, and broke it neatly into pieces. "That's why I named the dog after him."

Heather's eyebrows ratcheted up a notch. She and Justin had always wondered about that.

"After I lost poor little Fifi, I wasn't sure I wanted another dog. Then one day I just happened to be passing a pet shop. I saw Clarence in the window with his little paws up on the glass, begging me with his eyes to buy him and take him home. So I did. While I was taking him out to the car on his new leash, he picked up a stick in his mouth, and he wouldn't put it down. He took it right in the car with him, and when I got him home, he picked that stick up and carried it right up the steps into the building. He did the same thing when I took him for a walk after supper that night. By the time he got his second stick home and added it to his collection, I knew what his name would be."

Mrs. Grasso looked up at the cat clock on the wall, and

for a moment she seemed to be hypnotized by the huge eyes clicking back and forth in time to the switching tail. "I wouldn't worry about Justin and his coin flipping," she said. "It probably just eases his mind after all he's been through. Like I always figured with Clarence, it's good for a man to have a hobby."

Heather set the remains of her sticky bun down on her plate and wiped her fingers on a paper napkin. Her mug of rainwater coffee, half empty now and getting cold, no longer looked appealing.

Somehow this little chat hadn't done her as much good as she had hoped.

CHAPTER
10

Laurie was humming to herself the next afternoon while she used a big yellow sponge to wipe the counter in the day care center's kitchen. "Oh, I almost forgot," she told Heather. "There was a man here yesterday asking for you." She went on humming, then added, "He didn't leave his name."

Heather was watching Casey trying out a stuffed animal for taste over in the corner. "Well, was he looking for a place for his child?"

"No, I don't think so. He didn't look like a father, somehow. He asked why you weren't here, had something happened to you. I thought maybe he was a friend of yours. I told him about the fire in your apartment building, and he seemed real interested, wanted to hear all about it. I told him you were all okay."

Heather turned to look at Laurie. "Interested in the fire? What did this man look like? Can you remember?"

"Oh, kind of big. A bit on the pudgy side, what you might call stocky. Older, but not real old." Laurie placed the leftover juice in the refrigerator and hefted the industrial-sized jar of peanut butter back into the cupboard. "Had a real quiet voice. Looked like he didn't spend much time outside."

Heather gazed at the window over the counter, remembering the large, pale face that had hung for a moment just beyond the glass a few days ago like a ghostly full moon. Was this the same man? What did he want?

"It looked like he was sorry he missed you, but don't worry," Laurie added as she took off her apron. "He said he might be back sometime."

* * *

At the hospital, Justin suddenly jumped out of bed and began to get dressed.

Through thousands upon thousands of coin flips, he had been thinking about the events of the past few days. If someone was trying to kill him—and it was looking more and more as if this was the situation—then it obviously had something to do with the death of Professor Quint. And that meant the someone must be in his math class. And it was up to him to figure out who that someone was before that someone got him—and his whole family with him.

He paused, halfway into his pants, and gripped the rail at the end of the bed in both hands, woozy with the exertion of dressing after lying still for so long. He hung there at the end of his bed, weaving slightly like a river weed in the current, ignoring the curious stare of his roommate.

Well, maybe he was wrong. Maybe there was a break somewhere in his logic. Maybe—

Not a chance.

He pulled on his clothes, paced down the corridor, ignoring the annoyed calls from the nurses' station, and caught a bus in front of the hospital that would take him to City College for his Wednesday evening class.

He arrived early and took a seat in the rear corner of the room, behind the chair where old Sneezy always sat, so that he could see all the other students as they came in. He wanted to watch their faces. If anyone looked surprised to see him there, then he'd have his clue. The apartment fire had made the newspapers, but no names had been mentioned. As far as he knew, none of his classmates knew where he lived. So the only person who would *not* be expecting to see him there would be the one who set the fire. *Professor Quint would be proud of my logic*, he thought to himself.

Rachel and Stacy came in, deep in a discussion of Rachel's art class. She glanced in his direction as she made her way to the front of the room, but she looked irritated to see him rather than surprised. Remington Trask trudged in, and Justin noticed that the ratty old notebook was back in its usual position, clamped under his arm.

Fred Whittaker did have a slightly startled expression on his face when he saw Justin, but all he said was, "Oh, you moved your seat." The three younger guys came in, arguing about their predictions on the pennant race, threw themselves into chairs in the opposite corner, and went right on with their argument without ever glancing in Justin's direction. James Shaner stalked in, finishing off a packet of french fries which was still warm enough that the lovely greasy smell permeated the classroom and made Justin's mouth water.

The classroom was filling up. And no one seemed to

care one bit if Justin was there or not.

Harry King sauntered through the door, chatting with the man who sneezed, not a trace left of Monday's case of beginner's nerves. He trotted to the front of the room and faced the class, his eyes glowing happily in their separate fishbowls. "Well, good evening, everyone. How did the homework go? Are there any questions about probability before we launch into good old algebra?"

The young man in the Packers sweatshirt asked something about betting in football pools, and King demonstrated the odds on the board, making the bet look like something less than a safe investment for this week's allowance from Mom and Dad. The man who sneezed asked about the formulas that insurance companies used in their actuarial tables. Justin was amazed at the stuff that King seemed to have crammed into his brain, ready to turn into words and flow out from under that skinny little mustache.

"Insurance companies use statistics on thousands and thousands of people," King said. "Their actuarial tables are an excellent example of the law of large numbers. As you worked on your homework since Monday evening, did anyone come up with any other examples?"

"I've got one," Justin said. He stood up and paced slowly across the room toward the teacher's desk. Gripped in his long fingers so tightly that his knuckles shone white was a thick sheaf of papers.

Watching Justin's advance, King stepped back from the desk, his cheerfulness falling away from him like a discarded coat. As Justin kept coming, he backed up until his shoulder blades were pressed against the blackboard behind him. "You—um—have something to show us?"

Justin spread the papers out across the desk like an oversized deck of cards. Each sheet was filled with hatch marks neatly laid out in bundles of five, divided into two columns by a narrow space running down the middle, and each side was neatly labeled: *heads* and *tails*. Page after page, the hatch marks marched in their columns, hundreds, thousands of them.

"I flipped a coin 32,582 times," Justin explained without looking up. "As you can see, the law of large numbers is clearly demonstrated by the results. The coin came up heads 16,289 times, almost exactly half the time."

Now he lifted his head and looked out at the class. They all sat staring at him, the expressions on their faces ranging from wary to frightened to somewhat disgusted.

Silence blossomed in the room under the faint buzz of the fluorescent lights. At last King seemed to feel duty-bound to say something. "Well, that's quite an exhibition," he said. "In the last two days you flipped the coin—thirty thousand times, you said?"

"32,582 times," Justin said firmly. He ran his eyes over the faces of his classmates, searching, searching for some glimmer of extra comprehension, someone who *knew*. "I had a lot of time on my hands," he said.

*   *   *

It was hard, Heather thought, running the day care center during the day and coming back to Mrs. Grasso's tiny apartment in the evening. Over and over during the night she woke up feeling as if she were drowning under the heavy blankets on Mrs. Grasso's lumpy bed. Mrs. Grasso had insisted that Heather and Justin take the bed while she slept on the couch in deference to Justin's long frame. But Heather couldn't breathe in that tiny, windowless room under the rows of embroideries lined up like watchful eyes. And every time she woke, she lay awake for an hour or more listening to Mrs. Grasso's heavy wheezing or her constant trips to the bathroom, where her dragging footsteps would end in a roar of water and the riotous clanging and banging of old plumbing.

If only Justin would agree to let them go home. Martha and her family had moved right back into their apartment the next morning after the fire, and Martha reported that she soon didn't even notice the smoky smell, although her children complained that their classmates teased them about it at school. Heather was sure she could get their apartment cleaned up and livable in no time at all. She'd be so much happier there, even if it did mean living with—and wondering about—Hugo.

But Justin wouldn't hear of going back. He wouldn't say why. He just wouldn't hear of it.

She was worried about Justin. Once he had left the hospital, he had given up flipping the coin over and over. In his time off, he had gone back to following the pennant race. This made him seem like his old self at first, but soon he was sifting through the newspapers for statistics, making notes, checking the TV reports, with the same weird intensity that he had put into the coin tossing. Watching him in the evenings, Heather tried not to think about Clarence Grasso and the collection that became more important than looking where he was going.

She had other worries too. Casey was waking with nightmares, as if he were reliving the fear of the fire over and over again. Mrs. Grasso said it was natural for the age, but Heather didn't remember Sarah going through that.

And that man was spotted near the day care center several times a day now, as if he were hanging around, waiting for something.

She had checked with the parents of her children, and no one was worried about an estranged spouse going off with a child, so it didn't really seem like a case for the police. Heather wished she could talk it over with Justin and see what he thought. But the right moment to bring it up never seemed to come.

Actually, she and Justin never talked much about anything anymore.

*   *   *

Saturday came and Sunday and still they stayed on at Mrs. Grasso's. The old lady never complained, but Heather could tell that the pleasure of their company was beginning to wear a bit thin.

On Sunday afternoon, after a gut-splitting dinner of beef stew, homemade bread, and apple pie buried under gigantic scoops of vanilla ice cream, the apartment seemed smaller than ever for the five of them. So when Sarah crawled under the kitchen table after Clarence, thumping against one of the table legs in the process and sending Mrs. Grasso's favorite Statue of Liberty mug crashing to the floor, Heather put her foot down. "You're taking the kids to the park for the afternoon," she told Justin. "I'm going home to clean up. We're moving back in tonight."

"No, I really think—"

"The kids and I are moving back in," Heather said firmly. "I hope you'll come too."

To her surprise, Justin didn't object any further. Neither, she noticed, did Mrs. Grasso.

They were rounding up jackets and frisbees and Casey's backpack when the doorbell rang in Hugo's shave-and-a-haircut beat. Mrs. Grasso buzzed him in through the front door with less than her usual enthusiasm. It was obvious that she'd been looking forward to a bit of peace and quiet, starting immediately.

They could hear Hugo bounding down the hallway, his

long, sneakered feet slapping on the linoleum in gigantic leaps. "Wait till you see!" he announced breathlessly the instant Heather pulled the apartment door open. "I've got it all scrubbed up and ready to go!"

"Slow down!" Heather told him, eyeing the black streaks that marched across the front of his Mickey Mouse T-shirt and down his wrinkled chinos. "What are you talking about? What's ready to go?"

"Our apartment, of course! I've been over there cleaning all weekend! I washed the walls and the woodwork and the furniture—everything looks good as new!"

"What kind of soap did you use, Hugo?" Heather asked.

"Soap?" Hugo's face fell. "I should have used soap?"

Heather's stomach churned. "To the park!" she cried. "Hugo too! To the park. Now!"

"Take Clarence too!" Mrs. Grasso begged.

The park was only a block or two from Mrs. Grasso's building. Casey waved his arms and chortled with glee from his perch in the backpack on his father's back, while Sarah rode high atop Hugo's bony shoulders, and Clarence frisked about doing his best to topple Hugo by wrapping the leash around his legs. They walked across the grass toward the playground, which was already full of children climbing and sliding and swinging and racing around while a handful of parents watched the mayhem from nearby benches. In the distance, a group of people had dragged two picnic benches together and were busy unloading food out of an assortment of coolers.

Soon Hugo was pushing Sarah higher and higher on the swing. Casey started to fuss and whimper in the backpack, and Justin pulled him out and started tossing him in the air the way he always did to make the baby giggle. For once, it didn't work.

"Maybe he's thirsty, Daddy," Sarah called from the swing. Justin doubted it was that simple, but as there was a water fountain over near the washrooms, it was worth a try. With Casey clamped to his chest, he headed in that direction.

Casey did seem willing to try to drink from the glittering arch of water, although in his usual fashion he ended up wearing more of it than went into his mouth. When he seemed to have had enough, Justin raised him up—and found himself face to face with Harry King, who had just emerged from the washroom.

"Mr. King!" he cried. "I've been wanting to talk to you. I'm in your math class—"

"Monday and Wednesday evenings," King said. His tone was wary. *I know who you are*, it seemed to say. *You're the weirdo who spent two days flipping a coin.*

"Right. I was wondering—see, there've been some really strange things happening in my life, and I've been wondering how to figure out whether it's chance or whether someone is *making* these things happen, if you see what I mean."

"Uh, I think so, but I don't see how I can help." King started to edge away from where Justin was standing.

"Well, you're an expert on probability and all—see, first Professor Quint got murdered—"

King gulped, "I hadn't heard it was murder!" He was slithering sideways now toward the freedom of the open lawn.

Justin matched him step for step, sliding sideways with him, in his face. "See, first someone tried to run me over in the parking lot right after Professor Quint's funeral. Or maybe it was just a bad driver. Then something fell off the top of the building next door to mine and almost wiped me out. Did it fall, or was it pushed? Then someone tried to torch my apartment building. Was it aimed at me? Please, Mr. King, what are the chances? Lightning can't strike *three* times in the same spot, can it? What are the chances?"

"This—this—this is really outside my field of expertise," Harry King stuttered. His eyes widened behind the huge lenses, focused on something behind Justin.

"Hey, Justin!" It was Hugo's voice. "Sarah wants—" Stiff-legged, Harry King stepped backward as Hugo joined them.

As used as he was to Hugo's appearance, Justin noticed how exceptionally awful he looked that afternoon in his soot-streaked clothes. His signature high-top sneakers were more black than pink now, and the fuzzy neon lace in the left shoe was no longer any particular color. The right shoe was held shut with an intricate system of paper clips and a few twist-ties from bread wrappers. His hair, probably as a result of his cleaning operations at their apartment, had managed to bunch itself up to form two large dark lumps on his head which, Justin couldn't help thinking, gave him Mickey Mouse ears to go along with his T-shirt.

"Look, g-g-gentlemen, I—I—I really—" King choked.

"That's three times I could have died in just a few days," Justin went on. "So what are the probabilities that it's just chance?"

"Hey, little brother, is there a problem here?" a deep voice boomed very close to Justin's ear. Justin turned and found himself tucked up under the chin of a man who was Harry King all over again, only a bit older and a lot larger.

"We saw you talking to these two turkeys," another voice said, "and it didn't look like you were enjoying the conversation." Justin turned to face the second newcomer—and gawked. This face too was Harry King's, the same round cheeks and bulbous eyes, even the same thick glasses, but the body was huge and the hamlike arms hung loose and ready at his sides.

More men were striding purposefully toward them across the grass. They ranged in age from mid-twenties to mid-forties and in size from medium height to even bigger than the first two specimens. But as they approached, Justin could see that each one of them, one after the other, was basically just another version of his math instructor. They stepped into formation on either side of Harry King and ringed around Justin and Hugo.

Justin clutched Casey to his chest, shielding him with his arms. "I just wanted to know," he murmured, "what are the chances—"

"These are my brothers," Harry King announced, and with all this backup his panicky look had been replaced by his more customary cheerful twinkle. "You remember, I mentioned them in class. You're asking me about the probabilities involved in three events. So let me ask *you*—can you remember what I told you about the chances of there being *eight* of us?"

CHAPTER
11

"It's my dad's birthday," Harry King explained. "As far back as I can remember, it's been a family tradition to come to the park for a picnic, and even now that my mom's gone, we keep it up. Besides, now that everyone's grown, our apartment is getting kind of small for all of us to get together."

They were walking back to the double picnic table where a wizened little man waited for them, seated in a folding chair at the head. His face, Justin could see as they drew closer, was just another version of Harry King's, only older: the same huge eyes glowing in welcome over a wide, generous smile. *So, actually, there's nine of them*, he thought.

"Dad, this is Justin Cobb, one of the students in that math class I've just started."

As Mr. King nodded to Justin his arms reached out, and as if it were the most natural thing in the world,

107

Casey's round little body slipped into them. Casey gurgled contentedly and fiddled with the buttons of Mr. King's pale blue sweater.

"And look at this precious little girl!" Mr. King called out. "What's your name, my sweet?"

Sarah's voice was a whisper: "Sarah Angela Cobb."

"Well, Sarah Angela Cobb, I always wanted a little girl just like you, and all I ever got was all these boys! What do you think of that?" And Sarah was standing within the circle of his arm, leaning against his knee as if she'd known this gentleman every day of her short life.

"You hungry?" Mr. King asked. "My daughters-in-law always pack enough to feed us all for days, just in case we can't get back to civilization after supper." He grinned up at Hugo, past the dirty clothes and the wild-man hair and the goofy, don't-hit-me look, and grinned right into his eyes. "After all, it's my birthday."

Justin thought of Heather, struggling by herself to clean the apartment, of Mrs. Grasso probably cooking them another one of her enormous meals. But he needed this old man: his warmth, his wide smile, his confidence in all his sons, his complete acceptance of him. He needed to be part of this family if only for a little while. "That sounds great," he said.

Justin hardly noticed what they ate, but it was all delicious. "My sons all married good cooks," Mr. King told him. "I've just got to kick young Harry out of the nest, and my job will be done."

"Oh, Dad," Harry cut in, embarrassed.

"Tell me about where you work," Justin said quickly by way of rescuing him from more paternal breaches of his private life.

"Oh, I work for the American Signal Company. As I

told you in class, I'm in charge of sampling for quality control. We make turn signals for cars," he explained, "and send them out to car manufacturers all over the country."

"Cars," Justin sighed. "That's what I want to do—design cars. That math class I'm taking is just the beginning."

"Tell me about that math class!" Harry King said. "Was Professor Quint really murdered? There's such a bad feeling in that class! It just feels—I don't know why, but it feels *evil* in that room!"

"I know what you mean!" And lulled by the happy voices of the family around him, and the sight of his two children safe and contented on Mr. King's knees, he told Harry King everything that had happened since the night he asked to look at Professor Quint's calculator—the missing note, the questioning by the police, the string of times he almost died—everything.

There was silence around the table when he was finished, and he realized that the whole family—the father, the eight sons, the assortment of daughters-in-law, even some of the grandchildren—had stopped eating and talking and were turned toward him, listening. "So that's my story," he said, and a rumble of comment went through the line of brothers, like thunder in distant hills.

"What do you think?" Justin asked them. "All these accidents, the fire in my building—do you think they're just chance?"

"I don't think so," said the brother sitting across the table from him. "I think you've got a problem."

And again, the murmur of agreement rumbled up and down the table like a summer thunderstorm.

*   *   *

It was almost dark when Justin and Hugo, each carrying a sleeping child, arrived back at Mrs. Grasso's house. "Where have you been?" Mrs. Grasso fussed. "Heather's been calling. She wants you to bring the children's things and get back to your apartment. Here, I've got everything ready, and I've packed a supper for all of you—those poor children must be absolutely *starving!* Now hurry up and get home to Heather. The poor dear is probably frantic worrying about you!"

Heather was frantic but not with worry. "*Look* what he's done to our apartment!" she hissed to Justin as soon as Hugo was out of hearing distance. "He used so much water on the living room walls that the wallpaper is coming down in shreds! He used a wire scrub brush on the woodwork, and now the paint is all scratched! He—"

"Now, come on Heather," Justin said, "I know he made a mess, but he meant well. Besides, the landlord will give us the paint if we want to—"

"Who's got time to paint and hang new wallpaper? If you remember, I have two small children and a full-time job! And look at our furniture! Look at our couch!"

Justin looked. The couch, which had been a pleasant blue, was now a muddy gray color. The cushions were mottled in gray and black streaks, suspiciously like Hugo's chinos. When he touched them, the cushions were sopping wet. "Well—"

"Did you hear him back there at Mrs. Grasso's?" Heather demanded. "He said he'd been cleaning *our* apartment. That's what he said: 'I've been cleaning *our* apartment.' What is this *we* stuff? If he's not going back to Nellie, it's high time he found a place of his own! I let him stay on after he rescued you from that stuff that fell off the building next door, but now, with this fire—there's been too much going on lately for it to be just happenstance! I'm beginning to wonder if it's Hugo who's at the bottom of all this!"

"Hugo didn't kill Professor Quint," Justin muttered darkly. "But don't worry. I'll take care of things."

Justin didn't come to bed that night until hours after Heather had fallen asleep. "What's wrong?" she murmured as he crawled in beside her at last. "Why did you stay up so late?"

"I took the first watch," he said, "keeping an eye on things. Now it's Hugo's turn." He stretched himself out and buried his head in his pillow. "Don't worry. Everything will be fine. Hugo's on guard."

Heather sat up in the dark. "Hugo's out there—on watch?"

"Mmm." Justin was already falling asleep.

But Heather did not sleep again that night.

*　　*　　*

Justin sat dozing in his cubicle at Manning's Luxury Auto Sales. He'd been up half the night while Hugo slept, but he strongly suspected that Hugo had not made it all the way through the second watch—he came to the breakfast table looking suspiciously as if he had just waked up. For some reason, Heather too had been cranky and out of sorts with dark circles under her eyes.

"Justin, call for you on line two," said Penny Koch's voice on the intercom.

Justin pummeled his face with the heels of his hands, trying to wake up, then reached for the telephone. "Hello?"

"Justin Cobb?"

"Yes, this is Justin Cobb," he said, aware that his voice was still thick with sleep. "How can I help you?"

"Don't talk to them," whispered the voice at the other end of the line.

Justin was instantly awake. "Who is this?"

"Don't talk to them," the voice repeated, "or there might be a problem at the day care center over on Randall Street. There are a little girl there and a baby who could get hurt."

The line went dead.

Justin gripped the telephone receiver as if he could squeeze it back to life. *A little girl and a baby who could— Oh God, Oh God—*

"Mr. Cobb, could we have a word with you?" asked a voice above him.

Still clutching the telephone receiver, Justin stared up at the person who had spoken. Two blue uniforms filled the entrance to his cubicle: as if the telephone call had conjured them up, the same two policemen who had questioned him over and over last week were magically back.

The older policeman pulled out George's chair and dropped himself into it, then propped his elbows on the desktop and gazed steadily at Justin across the choppy sea of untouched paperwork that covered his desk. "We'd like to ask you some more questions about Professor Quint's death," he said in an even voice. "We feel that you have some information you have not shared with us."

"I—"

"We need your full cooperation this time, Mr. Cobb." The younger policeman had taken up his usual position behind Justin's chair. "Otherwise we may have to consider you a suspect in this case."

Justin stared wildly down at the telephone receiver in his hand, then dropped it as if it had scorched his skin. "I—I have nothing more to say."

"Oh, come, Mr. Cobb," the first policeman said in a

tired voice, "let's move things along. We all know that you are aware of how Professor Quint died."

"He was hit on the head," Justin blurted, "but have you thought that maybe he just fell and—"

"Interesting," the policeman said, his eyes never leaving Justin's. "I don't remember that we ever mentioned a head injury, do you, Officer Sawicki?"

"No, I'm quite sure we didn't, Officer Mosher. It wasn't in any of the newspaper reports, either. The newspapers have been quite cooperative in the matter of keeping the details out of the news for just this reason."

"They told me about it that night!" Justin exclaimed. "I've told you over and over—there was a guy and a girl—they called 911—and they told me—"

"It would certainly be helpful if you could ever produce this young couple," Officer Mosher said. "They have never come forward."

"But you have the tape of the 911 call! You—"

On the desktop, the telephone receiver began to squawk in a tiny computerized voice, "If you want to make a call, please—" As Justin stared down at it, the telephone cord seemed to writhe and coil around itself like a snake. *A little girl and a baby who could get hurt—* "No!" he shouted. "I don't—"

"You don't what, Mr. Cobb?"

"I don't have anything more to say!"

"Is that your final decision?" Officer Sawicki's voice seemed to press into the back of his head. Justin clamped his mouth shut and snapped his head up and down in a single nod. "Then I guess we'll have to take him downtown, won't we, Officer Mosher?"

"I guess we will." With a gusty sigh, as if he just couldn't understand why Justin was putting him to all this work, the older policeman dragged himself to his feet.

"I'm not going anywhere!" Justin cried. He tried to slide past Officer Sawicki, out of the cubicle into the relative freedom of the showroom, but the policeman's stocky body seemed to fill the space entirely. He spun around, wildly looking for a way out—could he jump up on the desk and over the partition? *The person who called—he knew the police were on their way! He's watching! He'll see them take me out of here! I can't let them—* The thoughts clattered uselessly inside his skull, while at the same time he was vaguely aware of Officer Sawicki's heavy voice droning rapidly through the recital of his rights. *I've got to get out of here!*

And then a sudden sharp *snick* cut the air as something cool and hard encircled his wrist. "No!" Justin yelped. "You can't! You can't make me do this!" His whirling thoughts burst into words. "You don't understand! He's threatening to hurt my children!"

Officer Mosher raised one eyebrow. "Who threatened to hurt your children? Professor Quint?"

"No, no! I don't know who it is!"

"Ah, another unanswered question," Officer Mosher said and sighed so hard that Justin could feel the policeman's warm breath wash over his face. Behind him, the other handcuff snicked shut. "Let's go."

And suddenly they were moving. Officer Sawicki's huge hand clamped onto Justin's arm, and they were moving out of the cubicle, across the glossy showroom floor, past the gaping receptionist and Tony and George and a middle-aged couple who peered at them over the top of a secondhand BMW. As they threaded their way among the new sports cars placed strategically by the front door, their reflections—two straight, stiff bodies in blue, one dark-suited body bent almost double in an agony of terror—danced alongside them across the brightly polished fenders and doors and hoods. The front door lurched toward them. In a moment they were outside, where *someone* was watching him being taken away to talk, to talk, to talk to the police—

"No! No!" he shouted at the top of his lungs. "No! I won't talk! You can't make me talk!" The words seemed to ricochet along the lines of identical cars parked in neat rows all the way to the street. Had the someone out there heard him? Justin's eyes rolled in their sockets, searching for a shape, a shadow, that would tell him where that someone was hiding.

"Cobb!" screeched a voice behind him.

The policemen halted for an instant to let the words hurtle past them. Justin swung slowly around.

Mr. Manning stood in the doorway of the showroom, his face purple. The tendons stood out in his throat as if they were trying to break free of his skin. His hands raised themselves in front of his face, the trembling fingers curled into claws.

"Cobb, this is the last straw!" he croaked. "Don't you ever come back here again. You're fired!"

CHAPTER 12

"What's the matter, Nellie?"

Nellie, who had just come in with the little squad of kindergarteners who were escorted directly from school to the day care center at midday, was visibly trembling. Her long braid swung in energetic arcs as she helped the children hang up their jackets and settle themselves around the knee-high table in the main room. She seemed determined not to hear Heather's question.

"What is it, Nellie?" Heather asked again. "Did something happen?"

Nellie whacked a plateful of peanut-butter-and-jelly sandwiches onto the table in the middle of the circle of tiny reaching hands, spun on her heel with a wide swing of the braid, snatched up the milk pitcher from the counter, and spun back again to fill the children's glasses. Heather stood behind Sarah's chair and absentmindedly stroked her daughter's hair as the child chomped a huge gap into her sandwich half. Eventually, Heather figured, Nellie would run out of things to do to avoid talking to her.

But Nellie kept her face turned away. She hung over the children, flopping extra half-sandwiches onto their plates as soon as the first ones disappeared into their sticky little mouths, refilling their glasses almost before they were empty. The long dark braid swooped and twitched and swung as if it were alive and had business of its own. At last Heather told her to let Laurie finish up and drew her by force of will into the office. "Now tell me what's got you so upset."

Nellie hung her head. "That man we've been seeing—I think he might have been following us." She looked up at Heather with dark eyes haunted by memories. "Ever since that other time—I keep thinking—When I'm responsible for the children, I'm always thinking someone's after them, so—"

Heather nodded. She knew what Nellie was thinking about. Five years ago, a child had wandered away from the day care center, and they had all thought she had been kidnapped—or worse. Nellie had spotted the child in a passing pickup truck and sent Justin in pursuit. He had found the child but came very close to getting himself killed in the process. It was something Heather and Nellie never talked about: they both knew that if Nellie hadn't screamed when she saw the truck, the child would simply have been dropped off at the day care center, and everyone would have been spared a great deal of danger and heartache. It hadn't been Nellie's fault, really, just bad luck that she had frightened away the driver of the pickup truck and the child with him. But she had never forgiven herself.

"That man—could he be a friend of yours?" Nellie asked. "Because he seemed to know Sarah."

Heather's head snapped up. "He knew Sarah?"

"He said, 'Isn't that Mrs. Cobb's little girl?' or something like that."

Heather was silent for a long moment, thinking. This man was coming too close, whoever he was, especially if he was interested in one particular child. *Especially*, she had to admit, if that child was hers.

She tried to visualize the pale, moonlike face she'd glimpsed at the window the other evening and the figure she'd seen silhouetted at the end of the alley. She really ought to talk to the police, she knew. If only things weren't so weird between Justin and the police right now. She wondered how long it would take before all that stuff about Professor Quint's death would settle down.

Well, the police would have to be called. "I'll take care of this, Nellie," she said firmly. "Thank you for your report."

Nellie turned to go, but Heather put a hand on her arm. "Nellie, as long as you're here—what's going on between you and Hugo?"

When Nellie raised her eyes, tears brimmed behind the black lashes. Heather realized there were dark circles under Nellie's eyes that she had never noticed before. "I haven't wanted to ask you about Hugo," Heather went on, "partly because—well, I felt sort of funny about it. But what happened between you? You seemed so happy when you were first married and right up until last week."

Nellie hesitated, then sat down near Heather's desk and heaved a gigantic sigh. "I think it's the baby."

"The baby?"

The tears brimmed over and began to drip gently into Nellie's hands, folded in front of her on the edge of Heather's desk. "I'm pregnant, almost three months. When I told Hugo about it, I thought he'd be pleased. I thought he'd shout and dance around, you know, and hug me. But he didn't. He just stood and stared at me for a moment, then ran out the door. And I haven't seen him since except for when he was in the hospital."

Heather dropped into the other chair. "Well," she said, "congratulations on the baby! I had no idea! Hugo said you'd thrown him out for being too sloppy!"

More tears squeezed out from beneath Nellie's lids. "When he left, I was angry and hurt. I yelled some things after him—I wish I hadn't. But he knows I want him back. I got my cousin to talk to him. He just said no."

Heather reached out and patted the back of Nellie's small, cool hand, feeling the wetness of the tears against her own skin. "You knew right along that Hugo's been staying with us?" she murmured. "You don't mind that we're harboring him at our apartment?"

Nellie shrugged. "I guess he had nowhere else to go."

He had plenty of other places to go, Heather thought, *lots of other friends. For all we know about him, he may have family right nearby. So what is he doing at our house?*

A soft tap sounded at the door, and Laurie stuck her head into the tiny room. "I'm all done with the children's lunch, Heather. Did you want me to stay longer and help out?"

"No, that's all right, we're coming." Heather stood up, then stopped to give Nellie's shoulder a final pat. "You were absolutely right to report to me about the man who spoke to you on the street," she said. "I'm going to call the police right now."

But as she reached for the receiver, the telephone rang. "Heather," Justin's voice rasped when she answered, "I'm at the police station, and they won't let me go." His voice broke in a frantic sob. "Sarah and Casey—are they there? Are they all right?"

*   *   *

Heather stood in the middle of the floor in her tiny office, stunned.

She should get a lawyer for Justin, but he said he didn't want her to do *anything*. He was acting so strange! She wished she knew what was going on inside his head!

Where could she turn? Justin didn't want her to go home. But she hated to impose herself and the children on Mrs. Grasso again.

Well, she knew one thing that was going to change! Before she could lose her nerve, she grabbed up the receiver again and dialed her own number. "Hugo," she said firmly when the telephone was answered, "it's time you found somewhere else to stay. If you're not going home to Nellie, you need to get a place of your own."

"But—" Hugo's voice sounded thunderstruck at this outrageous idea. "But I promised Justin that I'd help look after you and the kids!"

"That won't be necessary," Heather huffed, suddenly far more resolved than she had been a moment ago. "I am perfectly capable of taking care of my children and myself! Now, when I get home from work today, I'd like to find you gone!" She slammed the telephone receiver into the cradle so hard that it bounced out again and hung awry over the number pad.

She was suddenly aware of a presence behind her. She turned around just in time to see of flick of something dark: Nellie's braid disappearing from the doorway.

She picked up the telephone receiver and held it for a moment before replacing it gently.

Maybe tomorrow she'd tell the police about that man who'd been hanging around. Tomorrow, when Justin wasn't in their custody.

*   *   *

Partly because she wanted to do something—
anything!—to help Justin, and partly to put off going
home in case Hugo hadn't gotten around to leaving,
Heather loaded the children into the car when she closed
up the day care center that afternoon and went to call on
Professor Quint's wife.

She had found Mrs. Quint's address in the telephone
book. The professor's wife had been reluctant to speak
with her but finally agreed to allow her a short visit.
When she opened the door to her apartment in the tail
end of the afternoon, Mrs. Quint looked thin and
desperately tired. Her hair, graying at the temples,
gathered around her face in wisps, and her dark pink skirt
and sweater, a stylish matching set, were wrinkled as if
she had been sleeping in her clothes. Heather was very
aware of being in the presence of a woman who not only
had lost her husband but didn't know why.

The apartment was in one of the older buildings near
the college, with high ceilings and tall windows
overlooking the campus. The walls of the small living
room Mrs. Quint led them into were lined from floor to
ceiling with bookcases, and the bookcases were crammed
with books—books standing upright, shoved in sideways,
stuffed into every available inch of space. Sarah's eyes
were round as she gazed around the quiet, shadowy
room. "Is this the library?" she asked.

"No, dear," Heather said, pleased to note that the corners
of Mrs. Quint's mouth had turned upward in a tired smile.
It had been a good idea to bring the kids along.

"Mrs. Quint," she said, "my husband is being held by
the police for questioning in your husband's death. I
know that he had nothing to do with it. I think the
police know this too. I think they think he knows
something about who *did* do it, but he doesn't." Heather

stopped. She was confusing even herself. The professor's wife looked distant and in pain.

"Mrs. Quint," Heather began again, "someone is threatening my children, and I think it may be the same person who killed your husband."

Mrs. Quint looked at her as if she were seeing her for the first time. She examined her carefully over the tops of her glasses as if Heather had been some sort of interesting insect that had suddenly appeared on her window screen on a summer evening.

"Please, Mrs. Quint, you have to help us."

Mrs. Quint turned her face away. Tension crackled along her jawline and down the rigid tendons of her neck. "No," she said. "No, I don't."

For a long moment, there was complete silence in the room. Outside on the street Heather was aware of traffic moving, cars passing, and then a city bus grinding along its route. But inside the room it was as if everyone had stopped breathing, as if time had stopped altogether. Even Casey, as if sensing that something important was happening, stopped squirming to get down from her lap and sat gazing at Mrs. Quint.

It was Sarah who broke the silence. She stepped forward away from where Heather sat on the worn leather couch and paced deliberately across the expanse of paisley rug that separated her from Mrs. Quint. She stopped in front of Mrs. Quint's chair and placed her hand on the woman's arm. Mrs. Quint stared down at the tiny hand and then slowly raised her eyes to Sarah's.

"Please," Sarah said, "please can you help my papa?"

Mrs. Quint squeezed her eyes shut. Without opening them she asked dully, "What do you want to know?"

"The police won't tell Justin exactly what he's been

accused of. They're playing a cat-and-mouse game with him, trying to get information out of him about your husband's death. He doesn't have any information to give them, but they go on and on, toying with him. Maybe they hope that if they press him hard enough, this someone else will come forward. But no one has." Heather took a deep breath. "Mrs. Quint, exactly how did your husband die?"

Mrs. Quint's eyes opened slowly but she wasn't seeing Heather. Perhaps she was seeing her husband's body as it lay sprawled on his office floor that night he didn't come home after his evening class.

"It was his heart," she said at last. "Gus had known for some time that he had a bad heart. He tried for my sake to be careful—you wouldn't think being a college professor would be dangerous, would you?—but he had a tendency toward a hot temper, and he knew that he had to be careful to control himself and not get too excited. Well, on the night that he died, someone got him upset. The police say that someone was in his office and *hit* him—hit him in the face, here." She laid her hand along the side of her face as if feeling a wound. "Not with their fists, but with something flat, a book maybe." She smiled ruefully. "He had plenty of those in his office too. The person didn't hit him hard enough to crush his skull but hard enough to break the skin. Hard enough to startle him into a heart attack."

She sighed, more of a sob than a sigh, before she went on. "The police said that even then if the person had called for help, Gus might have been saved. It would have been so easy to call 911 and then run away. But no—the person went away and *left* him there, bleeding, dying. By the time the custodian came to clean his office and found him there on the floor, it was just too late."

Mrs. Quint turned suddenly and stared straight into Heather's eyes, her own eyes open so wide that the whites showed all the way around the pupils. "Would your husband do that? Would he leave someone to die?"

Heather looked right back at her. "No," she said. "No, he wouldn't. But someone did. And now that same person wants to hurt Justin—and our children." Quickly, Heather told Mrs. Quint about Justin's note that had disappeared from her husband's office that night and about the accidents and near-misses that had happened since.

Mrs. Quint listened without comment, as if the events were just a story about something that had happened far away to people she had never met. But as she walked Heather and the children to the door, she said, "Good luck to you. I have lost someone I loved very much. I truly hope the same does not happen to you."

CHAPTER
13

The police kept threatening to charge Justin with murder, but they never actually did.

They dragged him through an endless day of questions and more questions and then the same questions over again—to which Justin answered over and over again that he had told them everything he knew and that he had absolutely nothing more to say. They didn't like that. But even so, they didn't charge him. Along about their own suppertime, Officer Mosher suddenly announced that Justin could go home. For now. "But we're keeping an eye on you," Officer Sawicki said.

Justin didn't care. Someone else was keeping an eye on him too—someone a lot more threatening than the two of them could ever hope to be. Without a word, he walked out of the police station and went home.

Heather found him at the kitchen table, his math papers spread out in front of him, staring down at some sort of chart he'd written out. "You're home!" she gasped. "What—?"

"They let me go. What are you doing here? Why aren't at Mrs. Grasso's?"

"Oh, honey, we can't keep imposing on Mrs. Grasso. This is our home. We live here. We'll be all right." She put Casey down to crawl around on the kitchen floor, then stepped forward to look over Justin's shoulder. "What's that you're working on?"

Justin threw his arms out over the spread of papers and scrabbled them into a heap in front of him. "They're nothing!" he snapped. "Just my math homework! Nothing you need to concern yourself with!"

Heather, in the midst of bending down to give him a kiss on the top of his head, stiffened, straightened up, and turned away, the kiss unbestowed. "Are you going to your class, then?"

"Of course I am. Have to keep an eye on them, don't I? What would they think if I didn't show up? Huh? What would they think?"

"Your classmates?"

"*Yes*, my classmates! Who else? Now, you get on the phone with Mrs. Grasso. I want you and the kids out of here, do you understand?"

"But, Justin—"

Justin's eyes were like black holes in his face. "Please don't argue with me, Heather. I know what's best."

Sighing, Heather dialed Mrs. Grasso's number. The telephone was answered on the first ring with a loud and energetic hello.

"Hugo? Is that you?" Heather asked.

"The one and only!"

"What—? I mean—"

"I had to go somewhere, didn't I?" Hugo's voice was cheerful. He was simply stating a fact, assuming that Heather would agree to his assessment of the situation— as if Heather had nothing to do with his current state of homelessness. "Mrs. G was kind enough to offer me her spare bedroom. How are the kids?"

"Oh—um, they're fine, thanks."

"Tell Sarah that I haven't forgotten *Super Gorilla Goes to Mars*. Tell her we'll finish sometime soon."

"Okay—"

"Well, thanks for calling. It was really nice of you to check to be sure I'd found a place. You're really cool, you know that? 'Bye!"

The connection went dead.

"Well?" Justin demanded. "You're going over there, right?"

Heather felt as if her face were on fire. "Um, we can't, really. That was Hugo on the phone. He's staying there now."

Justin's head snapped around and his burning eyes fixed on hers. "Hugo? What's Hugo doing there? He's supposed to be *here*, helping out!"

In spite of herself, Heather let her eyes run over the kitchen walls, still streaked from Hugo's efforts to clean them—after a fire which he might well have set. *Helping out! Right!*

"Well, okay," Justin said, "if that's how it is—you'll be safe until class is over, and that'll give me a chance to figure things out." He jumped up from the table, bundled the heap of papers together, and stuck them under his arm. "I've got to go. I need to get there early and talk to the instructor before class."

"It's only 6:00! Wouldn't you like some supper first? Justin, *wait* a minute! I need to ask your advice. There's some guy hanging around the day care center. He scared Nellie, and—"

"Look, I'm sorry about Nellie and Hugo, but if Nellie's dating someone else, well, they're both adults, right? See you later." Justin disappeared into the living room, and an instant later the apartment door slammed.

"That's not what I said," Heather muttered. "It would help if you ever listened to me. Sometime you might miss something important."

*   *   *

Sitting in the classroom that night, Justin felt again like a visitor from another country—or another planet. He'd hoped to get a chance to talk to Harry King privately, but as the time neared 7:00 and there was still no sign of his instructor, his chances were plummeting. Now the other students were beginning to arrive, entering the room calmly, passing by Justin where he sat perched near the back, settling down in their favorite chairs as if going to an evening math class were an everyday event. Waiting for Harry King to gallop in, they chatted about the weather, or the World Series, or work, as if Professor Quint's death had happened in some other class, some other college, some other lifetime. *Obviously*, Justin thought, *none of* them *spent the day in the police station not talking to the police.* Justin felt different, as if he no longer belonged among them, as if he had been randomly selected to serve as a punching bag. Picked out to be picked on. Somehow less than human.

Careful to keep his head still so that no one would know he was watching, he slid his eyes sideways to peer at his classmates. Fred still had his pocketful of pencils— each one of them slightly shorter than when the class began. *He must rotate his stock,* Justin thought, *and use each one for precisely one hour before picking up the next one.* Stacy and Rachel sat in the front row, heads tilted together, deep in conversation. The man who sneezed was camped out in his usual spot beside the window. James Shaner sat reading a paperback novel. The three yahoos sprawled in the back row, one of them restlessly thumping his chair leg against the floor. Everyone was here, Justin noted, with the single exception of Remington Trask.

He was usually one of the first ones there. So where was old Remington tonight? Decided he was too smart for this probability stuff? Or had he stayed home to rearrange his sock drawer?

In the distance, the campus clock struck seven.

Nearer, the front door of Kelly Hall squawked open and then shut. Footsteps skittered toward them down the corridor. An instant later, Harry King blasted through the classroom, skidded down the aisle, and came in for a landing next to the heavy old teacher's desk, churning up a soft drift of chalk dust from the nearby blackboard. He grinned his wide jack-o'-lantern smile at the class and said, "Okay. Enough of logic and probability. Tonight we go on to algebra."

A sigh like a summer evening's breeze eddied through the room. They'd all been waiting for algebra, but now that it was here they weren't so sure that they wanted to give up the probability games they'd been playing and the funny sentences they'd been making up for logic.

King began writing number sentences on the board. The chalk emitted a piercing squeak, eliciting an answering squeal from Stacy. Fred winced, ducking his head perilously near his rack of pencil points. The man who sneezed did so again.

Behind Justin, the chair groaned in complaint as someone shifted his weight heavily.

Justin glanced around. Remington Trask's watery blue eyes looked steadily back at him. They were as blank as a lizard's eyes, offering no comment as to where he had been or what he had been up to.

How long had Trask been sitting there? How had he managed to get that flabby bulk of his into the room without Justin seeing him? With all the empty seats in the room, why *that* seat, right behind *him*?

Justin turned to face the front of the room again. It was probably just his imagination, but he thought he felt the hairs on the back of his neck stir as the faintest ghost of a warm breath washed over him from behind.

The chalkboard filled with x's and y's, plus and minus signs, numbers large and small, as King happily attacked its dusty surface with his chalk, chattering the whole time about positive and negative numbers. Justin tried to concentrate, to remember what he'd learned so long ago in Mr. Dogood's algebra class during his sophomore year in high school. He hadn't paid much attention then and he was having a terrible time paying attention now, with that whisper of warm breath playing across the back of his neck. He found his own breathing falling into the same rhythm as it came and went, came and went.

Concentrate, you fool. Breath. *He's not really breathing on you—it's just your imagination.* Breath. *If $x+2=5$, then x is 3, that's obvious.* Breath. *If $x-2=5$, then x must be 7, right?* Breath. Justin tried to keep his focus on the chalkboard, but all he could think of was Trask's fried-egg eyes staring at the back of his head. He shuddered right down to his shoes.

Why was Trask so late tonight? The question kept

tugging at Justin's consciousness. Did Trask even have a life outside of this evening math class?

Wait! What had Trask been up to? Had he been anywhere near Justin's apartment building? If Trask had seen Justin leaving at 6:00—if he knew that Heather was alone with the kids—

Justin leapt out of his chair as if he'd been burned. He lunged for his bundle of papers which exploded into a snowstorm of flying white sheets. He snatched them out of the air, crushed them together in his long fingers, and wheeled toward the door. He could feel the air in the classroom become electric with surprise. King's chalk had halted in mid-squeak. His classmates were frozen in the act of turning to gawk at him, heads awry, elbows jutting, lips drawn away from teeth in silent gasps. Justin bolted through them as if they had been a set of ice sculptures. An instant later he was pounding down the worn black-and-white squares of linoleum in the hallway, striving toward the big front door at the end.

The short trip back to his apartment building was a series of jumbled images: fumbling with the ignition key in his car, streaking through a red light at the intersection in the face of an oncoming truck, careening up the stairs to his apartment. In the hallway in front of his apartment door, he came to a stop.

Lying on the stained strip of brown carpet was Sarah's teddy bear.

Justin stared down at the familiar figure splayed on the floor. Sarah would never leave Mimi behind like that. Mimi was Sarah's comfort, her companion, her heart's true love.

His own heart felt like a clenched fist inside his chest. In the silent hallway, his imagination supplied the echo of Sarah's screams as someone ripped the bear out of her little hands and carried her away down the stairs and out into the night.

He stared at his own front door. He could not bring himself to unlock the door or even to call out. He knew that beyond that door the apartment lay silent and empty.

What should he do? He couldn't go to the police—they'd never listen to him. Or they'd think he'd done away with his family himself!

Oh, Heather, why did I ever leave you alone? Oh, Sarah, my darling little girl! Casey, my sweet little Casey! Where are you? In despair, he leaned his head against the door. The bundle of papers in his hand fluttered to the floor. *My whole family—gone! What can I do? How can I find you?*

He had to pull himself together! Maybe he could find a clue in the apartment—maybe Heather had found some way to leave him a message.

He tried the doorknob. Locked. He fished his house key out of his pocket, unlocked the door, and pushed it open slowly. "Heather? Sarah?" he called.

There was no answer.

In the silent front entryway, the closet door stood ajar. Quickly Justin pawed through the jackets. Heather's good coat was there, but her jacket was missing. Sarah's jacket and Casey's little blue sweatshirt were gone too. So they'd had time to dress for going out.

He passed through the dark living room into the kitchen where a light was still switched on. He glanced at the table and the counters, hoping against hope that Heather had left him a note. No note.

The bedrooms were dark and empty. With faltering steps, he paced back into the kitchen and reached for the phone. But who could he call?

Suddenly through the open front door, he heard something. Downstairs in the front hall someone was coming in. There were voices—a woman's and then a child's—*his* child's! Sarah!

Justin ran out into the hallway and leaned over the staircase railing. "Heather! Heather!" he yelled. "Is that you?"

Heather peered up the center of the staircase, a bag of groceries on one hip, Casey balanced on the other. "Justin? What's the matter? Are you all right?" The hallway echoed as she began to dash up the stairs. "Sarah, come on, hurry up, Papa needs us."

She rounded the railing and ran toward him. "What is it, Justin? What's happened?" She dropped the bag of groceries onto the floor next to their apartment door and turned to be sure that Sarah had followed her. "What's happened?" she asked again.

"Where were you?" Justin demanded. "Why didn't you leave me a note?"

"I went to the grocery store!" Heather said. "We were out of bread and milk. I didn't leave you a note because I thought we'd be back before you got out of class." She glanced at her wristwatch. "What are you doing home so early? It's only just past 7:30. You're all upset! Look at you—you're trembling all over! What on earth is the *matter* with you?" She bent down to pick up the papers from the floor.

"No, don't touch those!" Justin cried. He pushed her aside and gathered up the papers. "Come on, let's go inside. Sarah, pick up your teddy bear!"

"Oh, there you are, you bad bear," said Sarah. "I'd forgotten all about you!"

*　　*　　*

Justin was sitting, just staring at the kitchen table when Heather came into the room after putting the children to bed. She sat down opposite him and leaned her face in her hands. "Talk to me," she said. "What in heaven's name is going on?"

Justin didn't answer her.

On the wall, the clock ticked loudly into the silence.

"Okay," she said at last. "We'd better get to bed. We have to get up in the morning."

"I don't," Justin said.

"You don't? Did Old Man Manning give you the day off?"

"I don't work there anymore," was all Justin told her.

CHAPTER 14

Justin was sitting right where she'd left him when Heather and the kids got home on Tuesday evening, staring at his math papers which were spread all over the kitchen table. His eyes were bloodshot, and his hair was standing up on end as if he'd been running his hands through it over and over and over. He had a pencil clamped in his hand, but by the looks of him it had been a long time since he'd thought of anything to write down.

Sarah skipped over to his chair to give him a kiss, but as she approached him her steps slowed to a stop. "Papa?" He didn't lift his eyes from the papers. "Papa?" she said again, then slowly retraced her steps into the living room and turned on the television.

"Justin? Are you all right?" Heather asked. "You're acting so weird that you're scaring the kids!"

"Leave me alone," Justin muttered.

"What a day we had at work today!" Heather said, determined to make some kind of normal family conversation. "Nellie simply never showed up! She was all nerved up yesterday—there's a guy who's been kind of hanging around the day care center, and I guess it reminds her of what happened before when little Mandy Tate disappeared. Or maybe she's just gone to work for James Shaner and didn't bother to let me know."

"Can't you be quiet?" Justin cut in. "I've got to figure this out."

Heather gritted her teeth. "What on earth are you working on now?" she asked, fighting to keep her tone casual. How she missed the old days when he was forever sketching designs for sports cars! Now it was always these dreadful math papers. She sauntered in the direction of the refrigerator, trying to maneuver a peep before he bundled the papers up again.

But this time he didn't seem to mind if she looked at them. "I was trying to use one of Professor Quint's truth tables. He always said logic was the best way to figure things out."

Heather leaned over him and peered at the chart in front of him. Across the top of the paper were a series of headings: *Motivation*, the first column said, and then *Access* and *Weapon*. Down the side of the paper were names she didn't know: *Fred W*, *Shaner*, *Rachel*, *Trask*. When she scanned to the bottom of the page, she suddenly realized who they were. "Sneezy!" she said. "The man with allergies! These are your classmates from the math class!" She looked over the other sheets of paper that covered the kitchen table. Each sheet held a similar chart. Some charts had notations penciled into the columns. Some sported a big X slashed across the page. Most were almost blank. Justin had obviously been at this for hours. And, just as obviously, he was getting nowhere.

She dragged a chair around to his side of the table, sat down beside him, and picked up the paper he had been working on. In the *Motivation* column, the space next to *Fred W*'s name was blank. "This means you can't think of any motivation for Fred to kill Professor Quint? Who is Fred, anyway?"

"He's the man with all the pencils," said a little voice from the doorway. "Right, Papa?"

"Go back and watch TV please, Sarah," Heather said without looking up, "and keep an eye on Casey."

"Fred seems peaceful enough," Justin said as if there had been no interruption. "But look at this." In the space under *Access* Justin had penciled in 'Hide & return?' "The night that Quint was killed," he explained, "I was in the classroom waiting for Quint to come back after talking to Rachel. Fred waited with me for a while, looking at that calculator, and then he left. At the time I assumed he went home, but maybe he didn't! Maybe he waited in the hallway until Rachel left Quint's office."

"But why would he do that?"

"I don't know! That's why I left the *Motivation* section blank!"

"Oh, right. And he didn't have a weapon, either." She looked down the page. "Actually, according to your chart, no one had a weapon."

"Maybe they did. But the police have refused to tell me how Quint died, so I don't even know what kind of weapon to look for."

"I know!" Heather cried. "I went to see Mrs. Quint yesterday—"

"You did *what?*" Justin squawked.

Heather winced. "I thought maybe—I just wanted to help! Mrs. Quint told me that her husband died from a heart attack which was brought on when he was hit on the head. He was hit with something flat. Like a book!"

"Oh, great!" Justin sighed. "A book. The guy was a college professor! His office was probably *jammed* with books, all just waiting for someone to pick one up and smack him!"

Heather, visualizing the bookshelves in his apartment, nodded somberly. Too many weapons were just as bad as no weapon at all! "Okay," she said, still trying to keep him talking now that he had got started, "what about these others? The next one on the list is *Rachel*. I see you put a check mark for her under *Access* because you know she was in Quint's office that night. But what's this under *Motivation*? It looks like it says 'Pig.'"

"Quint liked to tell the women that they weren't as smart in math as the men. Rachel was really angry at break that night and said someone should put a stop to this male chauvinist pig."

"But this is Rachel Hylen, isn't it, who brings her son Allen to the day care center? She doesn't seem like the kind of person who would watch someone keel over with a heart attack and then just leave him there to die!"

"You're right," Justin admitted. "She's got a sharp tongue, but that doesn't make her a killer."

"The next person is James Shaner," Heather said, peering again at the chart. "I see you gave him points for motivation. Is that because he and Quint had a shouting match in public? And it made the newspapers? So you think maybe Quint said something that pushed Shaner too far, and Shaner followed him to his office after Rachel left and punched his lights out." Heather stopped with the guilty realization that she *wanted* it to be

Shaner who was responsible. If Shaner was discredited, his day care center would never get off the ground! "Maybe he hit him and then took off without realizing that Quint was having a heart attack," she added, compromising on making Shaner halfway to blame.

Justin shook his head. "I just don't know. He and Quint kept having these verbal battles during class over the finer points of logic or whatever. Quint would get heated up, but Shaner was always calm and cool. I had the feeling he really enjoyed a battle of wits, but he doesn't seem like the kind of person who would go physical. He seems like one of those real cerebral types, one of those people who hardly know they've *got* a body!"

Heather sighed and looked back down at the chart. "Okay. Sneezy seems to be out—"

"I've never heard him say a word in class. All he does is sneeze, but Harry King throws a lot more chalk dust than Quint ever did, and Sneezy doesn't seem to object."

"And who are these down here? You've got them all lumped together as *Packer Fans*. You don't know their names?"

"A bunch of young guys. One of them wears a Packers sweatshirt." Justin shrugged. "They don't seem to have much motivation for anything except sports and partying. I can't imagine them caring enough about a math professor to kill him. Even if he threatened to flunk them all."

"And the last one is *Trask*. Nothing after his name."

"That's Remington Trask. He's a real creep, but I have no reason to think he was even there after class the night of the murder." Justin shuddered, remembering the fried-egg eyes, the warm breath wafting across the back of his neck until it drove him nuts enough to send him careening out of the classroom the evening before. *Who was acting like a nutcase last night?* he asked himself. *Old Remington is sitting there minding his own business, and just because he's a little late for class, I go berserk and think he's kidnapped my family while they're down the block at the grocery store!*

"I'm sure Trask didn't have anything to do with Quint's death," Justin said. "He probably went home all by himself to his bare little apartment that night and stared at the wall until morning. He says he loves math. Why would he want to bump off his professor?"

"So that leaves you pretty much where you started, doesn't it?" Heather said. She flicked the latest chart into the air to flutter down and add itself to the heap on the table. She placed her small, square hand over Justin's long, slender fingers. "No wonder you're feeling so frustrated. You *and* the police!"

At the mention of the word *police* Justin snatched his hand away. "All right, so you can't help," he snarled. "Now leave me alone! What happened to supper, anyway?"

Stung, Heather stood up and finished her trip to the refrigerator. She'd always thought they made a good team. But after all they'd been through together, when he really needed help, he wouldn't let her near him!

"Papa?" said the little voice again.

Both Heather and Justin looked down at their daughter. Her small face was turned upwards toward her father's, her expression serious. She looked somehow ancient, like a tiny great-grandmother. "What is it, honey?" Justin asked.

"Papa, remember once you were telling Mama that when you're selling cars you go with Gus Reaction about people? That sad lady with all the books—she talked about Gus too. Was she talking about Gus Reaction?"

Heather looked confused, but Justin relaxed for a

moment and chuckled. "No, honey, her husband's name was Augustus Quint. She must have called him Gus for short. And what I was saying before was that I go with my *gut* reaction." He patted his stomach. "I just know in my gut about what people will do. Do you understand? Now run along and watch television."

But Sarah didn't leave. "Papa, remember that morning at breakfast when you were telling me about the people in your class?"

Justin nodded. When was that—two or three weeks ago? It seemed like forever, a different lifetime. But his little Sarah never forgot *anything*.

"Well, you told me that Remington person was going to go postal and kill people in a restaurant, remember?"

Justin winced. "Well, I didn't mean—"

"But, Papa, you *know* about people! You said someone was going to get killed. And someone got killed! Papa, you *knew*!"

There was silence in the room, broken only by a car horn bleating somewhere down the block. Then Justin reached out, plucked the chart off the heap of papers, and picked up his pencil. Next to Remington Trask's name, under *Motivation*, he penciled in "Creep." Under *Access*, he added the words, "The same as anyone else's." And under *Weapon*, he wrote, "The world's fattest notebook."

He stared down at his work with obvious satisfaction. Then he suddenly looked up at Heather. "What did you say before?" he demanded. "About someone hanging around the day care center?"

Heather's eyes widened. "Oh, my God! Justin, what does this Remington Trask look like? He's white, right? Really pale, kind of big and soft—"

"Looks like he crawled out from under a rock," Justin

confirmed. "Pale eyes, sort of flat, somehow—"

"Oh, Justin, why didn't we talk about this sooner? That's who's been hanging around the day care center!"

Justin jumped up so fast that his chair flew backwards and thumped against the front of the sink. "He's been stalking you? You and the kids? That's why I wanted you to stay with Mrs. Grasso! He's been calling me on the phone, threatening to hurt the children if I talk to the police. And what choice did I have when they took me off in handcuffs? I've been going crazy with worry!"

"Oh, darling, why did you bear this all by yourself?" Heather wailed. "No wonder you've been acting so strange! I thought you really *were* going crazy! Why didn't you *tell* me?"

"I couldn't be sure." Justin ran his hands through his hair again, renewing the wild-man hairdo. "Like last night, when I ran home because he'd come in late. You were at the grocery store, but I thought he might have—"

"Nellie!" Heather exclaimed. "Nellie wasn't at work today! Oh, my God, do you think he went after her? What would he do to her? Oh, Justin, we've got to stop him!" She leapt up, dodged Justin's fallen chair, and dashed toward the telephone on the wall. "I'm going to call the police!"

"The police!" Justin snatched up the paper he'd been working on and stared at it wildly, then crumpled the paper in both hands and lobbed it past her through the doorway into the living room.

Heather stopped in her tracks, her hand outstretched toward the telephone. "What's the matter now?" she cried.

"What's the use?" Justin asked. "You never really got a look at him over by the day care center, did you? You couldn't pick him out of a lineup. And no one knows who pushed that chunk of masonry down on me or who set the fire in the hallway."

Heather's hand sagged slowly to her side as she watched Justin turn toward the window and stare blindly down at the street. "Never mind logic or probabilities," he said. "Never mind gut reactions! The police want *proof.*"

His voice was flat, as if all the air had gone out of him. "And we can't prove a thing."

CHAPTER 15

There was no answer at the apartment Nellie had shared with Hugo. Heather called again and again through the evening until, with a rising sense of panic, she dug through an old address book and found the telephone number of Nellie's parents.

Yes, Nellie was there, Nellie's mother told her, but she didn't want to speak to anyone. Mrs. Ramirez sounded worried, and she kept the conversation brief.

Relieved but confused, Heather hung up the telephone. "Nellie's okay," she told Justin. "Guess it's nothing to do with Remington Trask at all. I guess she's just working for James Shaner now."

Justin, standing by the window, staring out at the street, offered no comment. Competition for the Little Friends Day Care Center was not an issue for him at the moment. His family's safety was.

"You go to bed," he told Heather. "I'll stay up and keep watch."

"Oh, honey, you need to get some sleep!" If only she hadn't sent Hugo away, Heather thought. There was something calming about having Hugo around, if only because he never worried about anything.

She wrapped her arms around Justin's slim waist and squeezed. "Promise me something, Justin," she said. "Promise me that from now on we're in this thing *together*, okay? None of this business of keeping everything to yourself so I won't worry. We've always been a team. We're in this together, okay?" When Justin didn't answer immediately, she gave his middle another squeeze. "*Okay?*"

Justin laid his cheek on the top of her head. "Okay," he said. "I promise."

*   *   *

When morning came, Heather felt as if they'd both been participating in a sleep deprivation experiment. Justin looked owlish from lack of sleep, and she'd been so restlesss all night that she felt as if she hadn't been to bed.

"Don't go to work today," Justin begged her as she was stuffing Casey's arms into the sleeves of his tiny undershirt.

"Oh, sweetheart, I can't stay home! Without Nellie, there'll be no one there but me most of the day!"

"Then leave the children with me." Justin's voice was dull, hopeless.

Heather looked up at him, at the haggard face, at the black circles under his eyes. He couldn't possibly stay awake all day. "No, honey, I'm taking them with me. We'll be fine. If I see anything weird, anything at all, I'll call you right away. Okay? I'll be really careful to keep an eye out."

And she dashed off to get Sarah ready for kindergarten.

*   *   *

So, of course, it was a frantic day at the day care center. One little boy tripped over a toy train on the floor and scraped his knee, and a new child alternated between crying for his mother and throwing blocks at the other children. Without Nellie's help, Heather was rushed to the point of exhaustion. *Darn that James Shaner!* Heather thought. *This is all his fault.* But in the back of her mind, one thought kept nagging: it wasn't like Nellie, even if she were actually quitting, to waltz away from her responsibilities like this. *Something is wrong,* Heather fretted, *really wrong. I wish Nellie had been willing to talk to me.*

She did snatch a moment to call Justin and reassure him that all was quiet—there'd been no sign of Remington Trask all day. It was quiet at home too, he reported, but his voice sounded as tense as ever.

How much longer can this go on? Heather wondered as she hung up. In her everyday environment at the day care center, all this stuff about Remington Trask seemed unlikely. Poor Justin was just worrying himself sick about nothing. Surely it would all blow over, and then Old Man Manning would probably take Justin back. If Justin was able to pull himself together and stop acting so weird.

She didn't want to think about what their life would be like if he couldn't.

The afternoon dragged on. Finally the last child was picked up. Heather left Sarah and Casey to play on the floor in the main room while she finished up some paperwork in her office. She'd better let Justin know she'd be late, she thought, and reached for the telephone.

The line was dead.

Irritated, she laid down the attendance report she'd been checking and rattled the button on the cradle. Still no dial tone. She sighed, making a mental note to call the telephone company just as soon as she got home, and went back to the attendance report.

"Mama," said Sarah from the doorway.

"Just a minute, honey."

"Mama," Sarah said again.

"Sarah, I promise, just as soon as I finish this, we'll go home. Now, please—"

"Mama, there's a man looking in the front window at Casey and me."

Heather was out of her chair and through the door into the main room so fast that she almost bowled her daughter over. Casey was sitting contentedly in the middle of the rug playing with a set of plastic rings. The front window looked out onto the late-afternoon street, the familiar shape of the telephone booth on the opposite sidewalk, a passing car. No moonlike face hung on the other side of the glass.

"He was right there, Mama," Sarah said, pointing at the side nearest the corner of the building. "He was just standing there, looking at us."

Heather fought to keep her voice calm. "What did he look like, sweetie?"

"He was white. Real white, like he never went outside all summer. Kind of fat. He had these googly eyes."

Oh God oh God oh God. How could she have been so stupid to be here all alone with the children? Justin's words from that morning so long ago kept echoing in her head: *He looks like the kind of guy who could suddenly go postal—*

Where was he now? Was he out on the sidewalk by the front door, or was he working his way down the alley toward where her car was parked? Could she still get there first? She grabbed up Casey from the floor, plastic rings and all, and gave Sarah a push toward the kitchen door. "Okay, Sarah, honey," she said briskly, "to the car. *Now.*" Catching the urgency in her voice, Sarah pattered beside her as she hustled toward the back door.

"Wait!" Heather caught Sarah by the back of her sweater and stopped to peer out the kitchen window. The alley, already in deep shadow, seemed to be clear. Her car sat alone, familiar, safe. She stepped toward the back door and reached for the doorknob.

The door would not open.

She rattled the doorknob, threw her weight against it. The door would not budge. In rising panic, she dragged Sarah back with her into the main room and ran to the front door. That too was jammed shut.

It was then that, once again, she smelled the smoke.

*   *   *

Justin was determined not to go to class. *Leave it alone*, he told himself. *You have no proof. You can't hang this on Trask any more than the police can hang it on you. Leave it alone.*

Soon Heather and the kids would be home. Heather would cook supper, and he'd read the kids a story, and they'd eat and eventually go to bed. And in the morning he'd look for a new job. He'd find something. Life would go on.

He paced the length of the living room, back and forth from one window to the other, looking out at the street, watching for Heather's car. He circled into the kitchen to look at the wall clock, then back to the living room. What was keeping her?

By now, his classmates would be headed for the dingy old classroom in Kelly Hall. Soon they'd be settling into their chairs, chatting, waiting for Harry King to scamper in and start teaching them math.

Math. Math he could use for designing cars. He wanted to be there!

A fury started in his stomach, expanded into his chest, pounded in his head until he couldn't breathe, couldn't think. It wasn't fair! This moron Trask had killed his professor, threatened him and his family, lost him his job, thrown his whole life off its path. And he was going to get away with it!

Justin couldn't prove Trask had done it, but he knew in his guts it was true. He had to find a way to force Trask to admit it.

As if he were walking in his sleep, Justin went downstairs, got in his car, and drove toward City College.

*   *   *

He spotted Trask lumbering across the campus, the ever-present thick notebook clutched against his faded plaid shirtfront. Justin slipped inside the front door of Kelly Hall and waited.

The door opened and the plaid shirt, the battered notebook, and one large, plump arm hove into view. Justin steeled himself and stepped forward into the gaze of those flat, lifeless eyes. "Trask," he said, "you and I need to talk."

Trask stopped in mid-stride, but otherwise he gave no indication of having heard Justin. Behind him, the front door swung shut with a grinding squeak.

"Look, Trask, I think you know something about what happened to Professor Quint. I think his death was probably an accident, but—"

Like a giant iceberg breaking off a glacier and slowly falling into the sea, Trask started walking away down the hallway.

"Hey, wait a minute!" Justin called after him. "I want some answers!" He lurched after Trask, ready to yank him away from the open doorway of the brightly lit classroom. But Trask didn't turn to go into the classroom. He glided past and on down the worn checkerboard tiles toward the darkened part of the hallway. Justin followed, murmuring, "Hey!" at intervals.

Trask wheeled left and pushed open a swinging door. When Justin wrestled the door open again, he saw just the top of Trask's balding head as the other man dropped down a staircase and disappeared around the corner at the first landing. Justin had no choice but to follow him down.

The basement of Kelly Hall was something out of the last century. A narrow corridor wound this way and that, studded with unmarked doors and lit by flickering fluorescent bulbs placed so far apart that long stretches of the corridor were almost completely dark. It was obviously nowhere that students were expected to be, but Trask seemed to know exactly where he was going.

It suddenly occurred to Justin that following Trask into the depths of the building might not be such a good idea. He slowed his steps and glanced behind him, considering whether or not he should go back. But just then Trask stopped short next to a right-angle bend in the corridor and turned to face him. "What do you want?" he asked.

Startled, Justin had to take a deep breath before he could formulate his question. "Was I right?" he asked. "Did you cause Professor Quint's death?"

"Yes," Trask said in a flat voice. "I didn't mean to. It just happened."

"What happened?" Justin pressed.

A gust of warm breath rippled over Justin as Trask sighed deeply. "I went to see Quint in his office. I had to wait for that woman to get done yapping about her homework assignment and leave. When I went in, he was packing up his papers to go home. I told him that I had solved the Yangton Algorithm."

"What's the Yangton Algorithm?"

"You wouldn't understand. Let's just say it's a mathematical problem that mathemeticians all over the world have been trying to solve for the last hundred years or so." Trask held up his notebook. "I have the solution right here. But Quint wouldn't even look at it. He just went on shoving his papers into his briefcase, and he told me I was an idiot to think that a beginning math student could solve any major mathematical problem, let alone the Yangton Algorithm." Trask drew himself up taller. "I'm not a beginning math student. I have been studying on my own for years, but when I solved the algorithm, I thought I would have more credibility if I had a degree in mathematics." He laughed, a short bark of a laugh, and stepped sideways to lean against the grimy basement wall. "Look where it got me! City College made me start at the very beginning, and my first professor wouldn't give me the time of day!"

"So then what happened?"

"Quint was shouting at me, calling me an idiot. He wouldn't look at my notebook. Then I lost my temper and hit him with it. That's all. He fell to the floor and didn't get up. I guess he had a heart attack or something."

"Yeah, that's what they said. Why didn't you call an ambulance? Why didn't you call for help?"

"Call for help?" Trask repeated, as if it was a new and unusual idea. "I never thought of it."

Justin shook his head. The guy was a true nutcase, not even attached to the human race! "So you were still in Quint's office when I pushed that note under the door?"

Trask nodded. "That's how I knew that you knew what I'd done. I warned you not to go to the police. I warned you over and over. But I saw you every single day telling them what I had done."

"But I didn't know you were there!" Justin cried. "I thought the office was empty! I thought Quint had forgotten all about his calculator and gone home!"

Trask's eyebrows lifted slightly, but the expression—or lack of it—in those fried-egg eyes never changed. "Well, if I'd known that," he said, "it would have saved me a lot of trouble. I wouldn't have had to try to keep you from talking to the police if I'd known you didn't have anything to tell them in the first place."

Suddenly Justin was once again engulfed in rage. "I was right! It *was* you! You dropped that chunk of masonry on me! And you almost got my family killed in that fire— You've been stalking my children! Why, you—" A red haze came over his eyes. His vision narrowed until all he could see was Trask's white, moonlike face. He felt an overwhelming need to get rid of that stupid, expressionless face. With a howl of fury, Justin launched himself toward the other man's throat.

Whenever he thought about it afterwards, Justin was amazed at the agility with which Trask stepped aside, allowing him to steam by like a driverless dump truck. Suddenly Justin felt Trask grab his arm and twist it up behind him, lifting him right up onto his toes. For someone who seemed so completely out of shape, Trask was incredibly strong! Pain shot through Justin's arm and shoulder, and he shrieked in agony and frustration.

"Well, now you know what happened to Professor

Quint," Trask said. "Now I have to figure out what's going to happen to *you*."

*   *   *

Heather wasted a few precious moments dashing back across the kitchen to dial 911 before she remembered that the telephone line was dead—most likely cut by the same man who had set the fire.

She stopped dead in the middle of the kitchen floor, willing herself to calm down, figure this out, *think!* The day care center had two doors—both of them blocked. There were windows across the front and along the side that faced the alley. She had no objection to breaking one of them—but that man was out there somewhere, and in the time it would take her to get herself and her children out through the broken glass, he could be on top of them.

Think!

She went up.

In the furnace room in back of her office, there was a trapdoor which led out onto the roof. Under normal circumstances, it would have been hard for her to get the door open and get two small children up that ladder. These were not normal circumstances. Pushing Sarah ahead of her, clambering one-handed and hugging Casey to her, she reached the roof in a matter of moments.

She stepped out onto the roof carefully, half expecting to find it engulfed in flames. Everything was quiet in the last slanting rays of the sun. There was not even a wisp of smoke, although the smell still lingered in the air.

She stole over to the edge of the roof and peered down into the darkened alley. Lights twinkled in the windows on the opposite side of the alley. No one was moving about.

She moved to the back of the building. Below her, her car sat nosed up against the wall. Beyond it, something was different— She craned to see in the deep shadows of the back alley. Then she saw it.

Someone had heaped trash from the dumpster against the back door and set fire to the pile. A few tendrils of smoke still curled upwards, but the attempt to set fire to the building had been unsuccessful. Like the fire in their apartment building, there had been more smoke than anything else.

Heather gathered the children and shepherded them back down the ladder into the furnace room. She unbolted a window in the kitchen and lowered them through it, keeping an eye out for any movement in the alley. The instant they were all outside, she dashed for the car. She didn't feel safe until they were out on the street, headed for home. She'd call the police from home, she thought. It would be much easier with Justin there beside her.

But Justin wasn't home.

She sent the children to play while she telephoned the police and described the situation at the day care center. Someone would investigate, she was told. She hoped they meant before morning.

In the meantime, she was listening for Justin's step on the stairs, his key turning in the lock on the front door. Where could he be? It was well past time for supper, and he'd said he wasn't going to class—

Then her eye fell on a piece of paper lying on the table.

It had been crumpled, then carefully smoothed out. She knew without reading it that it was Justin's truth table on his classmates' involvement in Professor Quint's murder.

That meant he'd gone to class. To talk to Remington Trask.

He'd *promised!* But he'd gone off on his own again! Practically brain-dead from lack of sleep, he thought he could take this guy on all alone!

Quickly, she dialed the number of her neighbor across the hall. The telephone rang—five, six times—but no one answered. Well, there was nothing for it but to impose once again on Mrs. Grasso.

Of course she'd mind the children, Mrs. Grasso said, and she agreed to meet Heather in front of Kelly Hall at City College. Frantic to find Justin before Trask did, Heather arrived at City College long before Mrs. Grasso could possibly get there, leapt out of the car, and dragged the children up the walk toward Kelly Hall.

It was easy to find the classroom, since at that hour there was nothing else happening in the building. The startled young man standing at the front of the room wearing thick glasses had to be the new instructor Justin liked so much. He nodded to Heather and gave a little wave of his fingers to the children, as if he recognized them from somewhere. But he hadn't seen Justin.

"I'm sorry," he said with a grin that stretched right across his face and made him look anything but sorry. "I haven't seen Justin. As far as I know, he hasn't been at the college at all tonight. In fact," he added cheerfully, "I have two students out this evening. We're also missing Remington Trask."

Chapter 16

When Mrs. Grasso pulled up near Kelly Hall, Heather was waiting for her by the door. Hugo leapt out of the passenger seat while Mrs. Grasso hustled the children into the back seat and drove away, leaving Hugo to see what he could do for Heather.

Hugo suggested that Justin and Remington Trask might have gone off to the Student Union for a cup of coffee and offered to go in search of them. Heather let him go, figuring that Hugo probably wanted a cup of coffee and a video game or two, and that this would be the last she'd see of him tonight.

She stood alone in the hallway of Kelly Hall, staring down at the worn checkerboard tiles and half-listening to Harry King's lecture in the nearby classroom, trying to imagine what Justin had done when he got there a half-hour or so earlier. For she felt sure that he had come to Kelly Hall. And she felt sure that wherever he was now, it had something to do with Remington Trask.

Further down the hallway the doors were all closed, and no light shone beneath them. *Empty classrooms*, Heather thought, *and professors' offices*. She wondered which one had been Professor Quint's office and wandered down the hallway to see if his name was still on one of the doors. It wasn't. Life goes on.

At the end of the hallway a staircase led upwards. She climbed the stairs slowly, listening, but all she could hear were her own footsteps echoing in the empty corridors above. She felt suddenly cold. Shuddering, she came back down to the ground floor.

Near the bottom of the staircase was a door that looked different from the others. She pushed on it to see if it was locked, and it swung open. Beyond it, a staircase led downwards.

She stood at the top of the stairs and listened. Far away below her there was a faint scuffling, like someone dragging his feet while he walked—or perhaps a rat. Again she shuddered and began to turn away, telling herself that Justin never dragged his feet. Not Justin with his long legs.

Another whisper of sound crawled up from below and touched on her ears. A faded murmur, as if someone had spoken down there months or years ago, and the sound had only just now found its way to the surface.

She had to find out what was making the sound. She pushed open the door and stepped through.

As she peered down the staircase, which grew darker and darker as it dropped toward the basement, it suddenly seemed important to leave some sort of sign behind, like the heroine in the fairy tale her mother had read to her when she was a little girl. Quickly she slipped out of her jacket and stuffed it into the hinged edge of the swinging door, jamming it open. Then she began to descend the stairs, step by careful step.

At the foot of the stairs, a narrow corridor twisted and turned as if working its way around unseen obstacles. A variety of doors, some extra wide, some almost too low to step through, lined the corridor. All were locked. The air was cool and dank and smelled of mold and old things.

The corridor drew farther and farther away from the overhead light until at last it turned a corner and another light pierced the dimness farther along. As she turned the corner, Heather looked back toward the staircase, as if it might fade away as soon as she took her eyes off it.

Ahead of her there came again the murmur of voices and the faint scuff of dragging footsteps. Heather stole forward, step by step, careful to make no sound although it seemed to her that her heart was beating so loudly that it must be echoing throughout the entire building, disturbing Harry King's class upstairs and giving away her presence to whomever—or whatever—was walking up ahead.

*   *   *

Justin tore at the hands that circled his throat. His legs flailed like the tail of a hooked fish. If only he could get his feet on the floor! But Trask held him pinned up against the wall by his throat, and Trask's wide, clammy fingers were pressing into his windpipe with the strength that only crazy people possessed.

Air— He needed air— He tried to hook his heel around the other man's ankle, but the massive legs were planted. The round, pale eyes stared into his without blinking, expressionless. A thought flashed through Justin's mind: *This is what Trask's face looked like while he was watching Quint die.*

Air—

Justin was more surprised than Trask when Heather appeared around the corner. With a banshee shriek, she threw herself at Trask.

He did not flinch. With that same amazing agility, he waited for her, then stepped aside at the precise moment and used the force of her own speed against her by reaching out one hand, wrapping his fingers in her hair, and smashing her head against Justin's.

Then he let them both crumple to the floor at his feet.

Justin struggled to drag air into his heaving lungs. He lay in a tangle of arms and legs, the floor cold and damp beneath him, fighting to control the spinning in his head. Heather lay sprawled partly across him, barely breathing. Just beyond, Trask's khaki pants legs paused a moment, walked away, reappeared.

When Justin looked up, Trask stood above them, impassive, waiting. In his hands he held a length of iron pipe.

"Remington," Justin croaked. His throat was so sore that the word made him gasp in pain. "What—"

"There are rooms down here they never use," Trask said as if answering his question before he asked it. He pointed to a narrow door in the corridor a few feet away. The door now stood ajar, and the space beyond it was as black as night. "They'll find you when they renovate the building."

"But—but, Remington, you didn't mean to kill Quint—"

"That doesn't matter now, does it?" Trask bent toward him. The big hand opened, dropped down past Justin's face, and seized his shirtfront. Justin felt himself lifted from the floor.

Squeak. Squeak. Something was trundling along the floor toward them from the direction they had come, something on unoiled wheels. Trask straightened up and stood frozen, waiting, the iron pipe clenched in his hand. Heather began to stir, and Justin pressed her to him with one hand. She understood and lay silent.

Squeak. Squeak. The sound came closer.

All three of them, Justin and Heather and Trask, waited for whatever it was.

Squeak. Squeak. Around the corner in the corridor came a custodian's cart, a push broom poking up from the front of its well-loaded trash bag, slowly pushed by a slender figure in blue jeans, a tattered T-shirt, and a tan cap set well back on his head. A tan custodian's jacket with the City College logo on the pocket was slung over the top of the toolbar on the cart.

The cart stopped. "Well, well," said the figure. "What do we have here?"

Justin held his breath. He pressed Heather against him, silently begging for silence. He knew that voice, and he knew she did too.

"He-e-e-y," Hugo said, bending down to examine Justin and Heather as if they were something interesting he'd heard about but never seen. He straightened up and offered Trask his hand in a high five. "You got those two! Great work! How'd you do it?"

Trask didn't answer. He looked at Hugo, his face blank. His hands gripped the iron pipe, ready.

Hugo took off his cap and scratched his head slowly and luxuriously until every strand of hair stood up individually like a piece of wire. "So," he said, yawning, "what are we going to do with them?" He swung his head around in an unhurried arc and stopped when his gaze came to the open door. "How about we stick them in there for the time being? They can't get out of there! Then I'll guard the door, and you can go get help." He yawned again. "It's about time I had a break, anyway."

Trask considered the suggestion for a long moment.

Then he suddenly bent down, grasped Justin's shirtfront, and in one motion dragged him to his feet. Justin tottered, dizzy, but managed to stand. In a moment, Heather stood swaying beside him. He put his arms around her, and she slumped against him.

"In there," Trask said, motioning toward the open doorway with his head. Justin glanced toward the iron pipe, then drew Heather with him toward the doorway.

He wished he dared to catch Hugo's eye. Was this really a good plan? If Trask did go away, Hugo could let them out. But what were the chances? Around zero. Trask didn't seem to care how many people he hurt. He didn't seem to care about anything. So the probability was that he'd smash Hugo on the skull with that pipe and leave all three of them to rot in that dark hole.

His mind felt as if it were boiling. He had about three seconds to come up with a better plan and communicate it to Hugo.

The narrow doorway came at them, and the black space beyond. In an instant they'd be over the threshhold—

He had to move *now!* Justin shoved Heather roughly to one side beyond the door. In the same instant, he jumped back and swung around, bracing himself to face the iron pipe.

And in the same instant, as if it had suddenly come to life, the custodian's jacket sprang up into the air and dropped down over Trask's head. Right behind it came the push broom, catching Trask across the chest and pushing him through the open doorway. Heather threw herself against the door and slammed it shut. All three of them piled themselves against the door while Hugo scrabbled through the tool chest in the cart, looking for something to hold it shut.

"I thought you'd *never* make a move!" Hugo panted. "I

was afraid for a moment there that I'd have to lock all three of you in there!"

"I thought you'd trust him to leave you there and go away!" Justin said.

"Not a chance! I wasn't going to turn my back on *that* guy!" Hugo said. "Don't forget, he's already nailed me once back there on your sidewalk! Ah, this will do it!" He lifted out a set of wrenches, and he and Justin set to work jamming them into the crack below the door and pounding them tight with the end of the push broom.

"But how did you find us?" Justin asked when they were satisfied that the door was as secure as they could make it.

"Heather left me a signal, of course!" Hugo gave her a big smile and a double thumbs-up. "That jacket of yours was a stroke of genius," he added. "That's what made me think of bringing along the custodian's jacket with the cart I found under the upper staircase. I thought it might be handier if it was loose."

Heather just stared at Hugo. It wasn't his quick thinking that amazed her—they'd seen that in action before. It was the fact that not only had he noticed the jacket stuffed in the doorjamb, but he had actually recognized it as hers. "I never thought you noticed what I was wearing," she said.

"Oh, hey, Heather, next to Nellie you're my favorite woman!" Hugo said.

Heather's smile was wiped from her face by a sudden ringing blow to the inside of the door right next to her head.

Through all that, Trask had never let go of the iron pipe.

*   *   *

The obvious next step was to go for the police. Hugo started to dash off down the corridor, but Heather stopped him. "After what Justin has been through in the past two weeks," she whispered, "we've got to take some precautions. We have to be sure we have a witness the police will believe."

They agreed on Harry King, and Heather managed to convince him to leave his class and steal silently along the corridor with her to where Hugo and Justin waited, shivering slightly, in front of a door which had been wedged shut. "What's going on?" King asked.

Justin held his fingers to his lips. Then he called out, "Hey, Remington, there *you* are locked up where you wanted to put *me*! What do you think of that?"

There was a stony silence beyond the door.

"Hey, Trask," Justin tried again, "how come you didn't just bash my head in like you bashed Professor Quint?"

There was still no sound from behind the door. King began to look edgy, as if he suddenly remembered that he was outnumbered—a long way from help—by people who had been acting very strange lately. *I'll bet he wishes he had three or four of his brothers with him*, Justin thought.

He racked his brain for something that would push Trask over the edge. "Well, I guess it served Professor Quint right," he said, "since he didn't bother to look at that notebook of yours."

He waited. They all four waited, staring at the closed door. Then King began to sidle away, back in the direction he had come from. "Sorry, folks, but I'd better get back to class," he murmured.

Suddenly there was a sound from behind the door. King stopped where he was as if he'd been flash-frozen to the floor.

The sound didn't take the form of words. It was a soft sound, muffled, infinitely sad. They realized all at once that Trask was weeping.

But it was not Quint that he was weeping for. It was for his beautiful solution to the Yangton Algorithm.

"All I wanted to do was show it to him," Trask sobbed in frustration and fury, "but he never gave me a chance."

CHAPTER 17

At the police station, Officer Mosher slumped over his computer keyboard, picking away at the keys with his two index fingers. He craned his neck to squint up at the screen, fighting to line up the bottom half of his glasses with the part of his report he was trying to look at. "Hate the darned things," he muttered, leaving Heather and Justin to wonder if he meant computers or bifocals or both.

Officer Sawicki stood behind his chair, flexing the muscles across his back while he peered over Mosher's shoulder at the computer screen. He stood on the balls of his feet, shifting his weight from one foot to the other, nodding in satisfaction as each sentence of the report came onto the computer screen as if he and Officer Mosher could take complete credit for how everything had worked out. Officer Mosher just looked as if he wanted to get the report done and go home.

Heather found a telephone and called Mrs. Grasso. "Don't worry about a thing," Mrs. Grasso told her. "I'll tuck the children into bed right here. They'll be fine. And that reminds me—when you get here to pick them up, you can admire Hugo's work."

"Hugo's work?"

"He hasn't told you what he's been doing here at my apartment? Well, we'll just let it be a surprise. I'll see you later!"

Heather didn't give the conversation any more thought until they were in the car headed across town to fetch the children and Hugo in the backseat started to hum. When she glanced back at him, he looked just as pleased with himself as Officer Sawicki had been. Heather shrugged. Whatever the surprise was, they'd soon find out.

In fact, there was a surprise for Hugo too.

The first thing they were aware of as they walked into the kitchen was how much brighter everything looked. Justin looked around to see if Mrs. Grasso had installed some extra light fixtures. Heather thought it might be just bigger light bulbs. Their heads swiveled as they tried to figure it out, and then it hit them both at the same moment. "New wallpaper!" Heather squealed.

Gone were the dingy little drum-and-bugle motifs that had marched diagonally across the kitchen walls. In their place were tiny sprigs of green against a cheery butter-yellow background. "I like it!" Justin said.

The living room walls were freshly painted in a pale green, the woodwork neatly decked out in a contrasting ivory. "Someone has certainly done a nice job," Heather said.

The bedroom had been redone too. The rows of staring picture frames were gone. The walls that encircled the bed where the children lay peacefully sleeping were lush with violets and rosebuds. And on the foot of the bed sat Nellie.

"Mrs. Grasso called me to see the work you've been doing," Nellie said to Hugo. "And she told me I had to apologize to you, Heather, for leaving you alone at the day care center. I felt terrible about it, but that Mr. Trask said he'd hurt the children if I so much as talked to you again!"

Heather's head was spinning. "That great big slug was *everywhere*, wasn't he?" she cried, shuddering. "We thought we were watching for him, but we never knew how thoroughly he was watching *us!*" Then a new thought struck her. "What did you say just then, Nellie? This room is *Hugo's* work?"

"Yeah." Hugo tried to make his tone casual, but it was difficult when he was wriggling all over with pleasure like a tail-wagging dog. "I felt really bad about what I'd done to your apartment after the fire, so Mrs. Grasso taught me how to paint and hang wallpaper, and she let me practice on her apartment." He looked over at Heather, his eyes wide with enthusiasm. "I think I'm ready to work on your place now!"

Heather looked around the room. His sweatshirt was hung up—on the bedpost, true, but it was hung up. His computer magazines were heaped on the bedside table, although one or two had already slid to the floor. Perhaps Hugo was trainable after all! After all the evil thoughts she'd had about him over the past week! Only his good old pink high-top sneakers maintained their independence, abandoned heel-to-toe smack in the middle of the floor.

"I really like this wallpapering stuff!" Hugo said. "That Harry King guy said that a couple of his brothers have an interior decorating business. I'm going to call them tomorrow and see if maybe they're looking for help."

When Heather turned to look at Hugo, he was standing with his arms around Nellie and his neck curved down so that his chin rested on the top of her head. "I was so nervous about the baby," he said. "I've never lived around little kids. I had to find out if I could do it. That's why I went to stay with Justin and Heather."

He gazed down fondly at Sarah and Casey, who lay curled around each other, flushed with sleep. Casey stirred, pushing back the blanket with his fat little arms, and Hugo bent down and gently covered him again. "You know what? I think I really *like* kids!" he told Nellie. "If you'll have me back, I'm sure going to try."

For an answer, Nellie buried her head against his chest. He wrapped the long, dark braid loosely around his hand and held her to him.

*   *   *

The week drew to a close. Heather had thought now that Remington Trask was in custody and the police were leaving Justin alone, life would get back to normal. And normal meant Justin should be getting up and going to work every morning. But he showed no signs of returning to his job at Manning's Auto Sales.

"Have you talked to Mr. Manning?" she asked on Friday morning as she spooned cereal into Casey's open mouth. "If he's read the newspapers, I'm sure he realizes now that it was all a mistake."

"There is no way I'm going to beg Old Man Manning for my job back," Justin said. "There is not enough money in the world to make it worthwhile for me to go back to that place." And he went back to staring morosely into his coffee mug.

Heather gazed at the little bald spot on the top of his

head for a long moment. Then she pushed Casey's cereal bowl across the table to Justin, put the spoon in Justin's hand, and went off to see how Sarah was doing at combing her hair.

She came home that evening bursting with news. "You'll never guess who showed up at the day care center this afternoon!" she said. "James Shaner!"

Justin looked up from his newspaper. "Shaner? From my math class? What did he want?"

Heather had yanked open a cupboard door and pulled out a box of Hamburger Helper. "He stood there like he owned the place, like some rich old businessman with that row of earrings in his ear—he must have eight or ten of them! Some of the children just stared and stared. And he said—" She held the box up in front of her as if she were reading from a set of notes and pitched her voice low to imitate Shaner's steely tone. "He said, 'Students for a Fair Shake has been successful in convincing City College to establish a day care center at Eastman Hall. However, the Day Care Committee has been rethinking the whole issue, Mrs. Cobb, and we feel it would be best at the present moment to scale our plans down a bit.'

"The guy talks like he's reading out of an encyclopedia!" Heather said, tossing down the box and returning to her own voice. "Anyway, he wants *us* to set up an evening babysitting service at Eastman Hall for people who just come to the night classes, and would it be all right if they put up posters in the Student Union referring day students to Little Friends Day Care Center? How about *that*?" She rummaged in the freezer section of the refrigerator and brought out a package of hamburger and a bag of frozen peas. "So Nellie is going to work half-time at Little Friends and half-time over at the Student Union running the evening child care. I'll miss her in the mornings—I never realized how much I counted on her until she was out those two days—but I'm going to hire another full-time person so we don't get stuck every time someone's out sick. It looks like we'll have plenty of work!" she crowed and slapped the slab of hamburger into the microwave to thaw.

Justin sat with the newspaper spread out in front of him on the table, still trying to work through this sudden change in Shaner's status. Two days ago, James Shaner had been Heather's favorite suspect in a murder case. Tonight he was a household hero.

He shook his head and went back to his newspaper.

The weekend passed. Justin spent most of his time with his head buried in the newspaper. Heather peeked over his shoulder from time to time, hoping that he was checking out the want ads, but he was usually in the sports section, poring over the statistics on the pennant race.

On Saturday morning, Hugo came over with a serene Nellie in tow to show them wallpaper samples and paint chips. As he spoke of complementary colors and washable wallpapers and the advantages and disadvantages of latex paint, Justin and Heather just sat and stared at him. They had never before heard Hugo speak sentence after sentence on the same topic without flying off onto another subject. Who would have ever thought that this wild-man computer jockey would find that his real vocation was hanging wallpaper?

Heather sighed. If only Justin could be so lucky and find something he wanted to do.

The idea of a house with a yard for the kids was becoming more and more of a distant dream. They could never get a mortgage on just her salary. When he was working for Manning, there hadn't been much of a future, but at least it was a paycheck coming in . . .

She didn't want to say anything to Justin. She thought of poor Mrs. Quint and that pathetic, lonely Remington Trask now sitting in a jail cell, and she decided to count her blessings. At least she had her family.

*   *   *

On Sunday afternoon the telephone summoned Heather from the lunch dishes. "It's Mrs. G again," she told Justin with her hand clamped over the receiver. "You know, the poor old thing's got an empty nest all over again. We really ought to do something for her."

Justin folded his newspaper. "I feel like getting out. Let's take her to the park."

As the five of them strolled across the lawn, Justin discovered that Sunday afternoon picnic-in-the-park time seemed to be a regular thing for the King family. They weren't all there, but with the family resemblance and the way they were constantly milling around, it was impossible to count them anyway.

The father sat in his battered lawn chair at the head of his table like a tiny king on his throne, smiling that jack-o'-lantern smile at his sons, daughters-in-law, and grandchildren alike as if every single one of them delighted him.

"Hey, there!" one of the larger brothers hailed them as they passed with Mrs. Grasso. "Aren't you friends of Hugo's? He's just started with us in our interior decorating business, and I never saw a guy catch on so fast!"

"Yeah!" said a slightly smaller brother, grinning from ear to ear. "It's like the guy's in love! He's going to need some work in learning how to clean up after himself, but he can paint trim slick as anything."

Heather smiled at the pair of enormous smiles and turned around to look for her family. Justin had walked off across the lawn, deep in conversation with Harry. The elder Mr. King was holding Sarah on one knee and was reaching up to take Casey out of Mrs. Grasso's arms. He said something to Mrs. Grasso that made her smile down at the ground and blush like a schoolgirl. There was nothing for Heather to do but sit down at the picnic table with a few of the daughters-in-law and relax for a bit.

Suddenly Justin came rocketing back toward her across the grass on his long legs. "Heather! Guess what! Harry says there's a position opening up in his lab for a technician! He says I'd be qualified! And they'd set the schedule up so I could go on with my college courses!" He grabbed her up off the bench and whirled her around. "I feel as if I'm finally on my way! They're just working on turn signals, but at least that's part of a car! And someday I'll be working on the whole car, I can just feel it! I've got a future now! We can get that house— Oh, this is going to be great!"

"I thought you'd given up on the idea of getting a house!" Heather said as soon as she could catch her breath. "I thought that we'd always live in an apartment, and that you would work for Old Man Manning for the rest of your life!"

"Not a chance!" Justin laughed. "Nothing can stop us now! We're on our way!"